Look

LOOKS Perfect

kim moritsugu

GOOSE LANE

Published by Goose Lane Editions with the assistance of the Canada
Council, 1996.

This book is a work of fiction. Names, characters, places and incidents
are either the product of the author's imagination or are used fictitiously. Any
resemblance to actual events or locales or persons, living or dead, is entirely
coincidental.

Edited by Laurel Boone.
Cover illustration: "Wash drawing of Halston Knitwear," 1984 (detail), by
Tony Viramontes. Originally published in *Fashion Illustration Today* (Thames
and Hudson Ltd., 1987, 1994).
Book design by Julie Scriver.
Printed in Canada by Gagné Printing.
10 9 8 7 6 5 4 3 2

Canadian Cataloguing in Publication Data

Moritsugu, Kim, 1954-
    Looks perfect
    ISBN 0-86492-196-9

I. Title.

PS8576.075L66 1996   C813'.54   C96-950032-7
PR9199.3.M67L66 1996

Goose Lane Editions
469 King Street
Fredericton, NB
CANADA E3B 1E5

To Simon and Michael

and to Ehoud

Acknowledgements

For his salient teaching and generous moral support, I am indebted to Paul Quarrington.

For very graciously allowing me to watch her at work, I thank Catherine Franklin, Fashion Director of *Toronto Life Fashion* magazine.

For their invaluable advice, I thank Oakland Ross, Lawrence Hill, and Victoria Ridout.

For helping me sail the fictional Flying Dutchman, I thank Sally Hill.

For recommending that Max sleep naked, and other equally wise editorial suggestions, I am forever grateful to Laurel Boone.

And thanks to Meg Taylor, Suzi Roher, Shelley Black, Joan Harting Barham, Darina Phillips, Suzy Tan, Mary Li, Rolande Herman, Louise Moritsugu, and David Moritsugu.

Chapter One

So there I was, Paris-in-the-spring for the fall ready-to-wear, sitting in the back row at the St. Amand show, notebook open, pen poised. There I was, exhausted but fuelled by the buzz, eager to see what Jean-Luc would send down the runway this time. If the show ever got started.

I checked my watch and scoped the room for the nth time. On the other side of the runway, an intrepid buyer was pleading with the misguided soul in the huge-brimmed hat to take it off. Over by the entrance doors, a gate-crashing fashion groupie was being escorted out by security. And several leagues in front of me, the fashion press celebrities were all accounted for, lined up in the first row.

But hey now. Who was this attractive man in black strolling toward a front-row seat? I watched him raise a hand and run long fingers through wavy hair. I gazed at his largish nose, ruddy skin, light eyes, and felt a sharp twinge of attraction. I turned to Marni Cohen — my editor, my boss — to ask who he was.

But Marni was deep in gossip with the fashion editor of the *Chattanooga Times*, on her other side. They were discussing Kayla, the hot new model that year, the runway's current star. I didn't interrupt.

The room was packed and hot. Women around me fanned themselves with their programs. Over in the photographers' section, a scuffle broke out over tripod real estate. The photographers not pushing and shoving started singing "The Marseillaise." I rolled up my sleeves, wiped the sweat off my upper lip, and yearned for the breezy spring streets outside.

The house lights came down at last, Arrested Development bounced out of the sound system, and a cheer went up. I slipped on my sunglasses and clapped with the rest of the audience at the sight of Kayla, spotlit on stage.

Her black buzzcut was covered with a curly orange wig, and the tattooed chains which adorned the skin across her collarbone weren't visible under the high neck of the dress she wore — a clinging cashmere number, in shades of autumn leaves. On her long legs were moss-coloured tights, on her feet brown suede boots. To look at her in that wood-nymph get-up, you'd never know she was a seventeen-year-old punker with a sweet face and excess attitude.

I watched her stride down the runway, watched her turn and stop halfway, at the perfect focal point for the important photographers occupying the choice positions along the sides.

She shifted her hip, twirled, struck a pose, and winked at someone in the front row. The someone waved back. I leaned to the left, then to the right, straining to see the object of her affection, and recognized the wavy hair of the good-looking man I'd noticed before. Who *was* this guy?

When the show ended, I tapped Marni on the arm. "Hey, Marni, see that man up there in the front row? Straight ahead of us? Who is he, do you know?"

She wrote two more lines in her book before lifting her head. "What are you asking me?"

"Who's that guy?" I pointed with a bent finger. "There, reddish hair, standing talking to that blonde woman."

"That," she said, "is Brian Turnbull. He owns *Fashion Folio* and several other books in Asia, out of Sydney, Australia. Surely you've heard of him. He's an arrogant jerk. Now is that all? I'd like to finish up here."

"Okay, okay. That's all." I shifted in my chair and stared some more at Brian. I'd never seen him before that I could recall in my three years of attending the European and New York collections as fashion editor of *Panache*. No, I was pretty sure I'd remember laying eyes on someone with that rugged look, that air of having been there and back and of having been laid a couple of hundred times on the way.

I watched Brian grin at the blonde and admired his laugh lines. The woman walked off, and Brian's gaze swept the room. Before I could look away, it met my stare. I blushed and became engrossed in burrowing in my purse. When I was brave enough to peek up again a minute later, he'd turned his back, was heading backstage. To see Kayla, no doubt.

Marni stood beside me. "Do you think we could go now, Rosemary?"

I jumped up. "Oh, yeah. Sure. I'm ready. You ready?"

Go back eight years. Picture me: long student hair, an Indian-print dress, ten silver bangles on each wrist, no makeup. Then see Marni: dark hair, cut not blunt but sharp, in a chin-length bob that shows off her jaw, clenched like she grits her teeth all night. Every night. Unlike me, she's garbed in something chic and black. Her face is pale, her lipstick dark red. Scary.

It was my first day at *Panache*. I'd been hired as a lowly editorial assistant, reporting to the assistant fashion editor. But, around mid-day, it was part of Marni's job as fashion editor to give me a pep talk.

She sat up very straight, her hands folded on her desk. "How's it going so far?" she said. Her grey eyes did not smile.

"It's a bit overwhelming — "

"You'll sort it out. All we ask is that you're dedicated and co-operative, and that you work hard. I'm told you graduated in journalism?"

"Yes. From Carleton." No reaction. "University. With a minor in film studies."

She smiled now, even the eyes, in a catlike way I would grow to recognize as an expression of amusement. "Film studies."

I blathered on about my degree as it dawned on me that neither my major nor my minor could be considered good job qualifications at *Panache*. Like probably what these fashion nuts were looking for was someone who'd worked in retail or for a garment manufacturer — someone who knew anything at all about the business, say.

"I'm sure you'll do fine," she said.

"I hope so."

"As long as you don't think you're too good for the job. Some of your predecessors had expectations that didn't match our reality."

"No great expectations here," I said, and rued the day I'd let my dad arrange an interview with his friend Campbell Cameron, the publisher of *Panache*. An interview which had led to this job.

"Let me explain what's required," Marni said, "so there'll be no misunderstandings."

I listened to her tell me that no task was too simple, no assignment too menial, and I checked out her office decor: the colour charts on the desk, the framed magazine covers on the wall, the contact sheets piled up in the In tray. Funny how nothing looked at all how I'd imagined it the night before, when I'd lain in bed, waiting for sleep, and visualized an office peopled with Rosalind Russell in one corner, in a padded-shoulder suit and rakish hat, smoking cigarettes and making wise, and Kay Kendall in the other, tossing bolts of fabric about and shouting, "Think pink!"

Now, instead, here was Marni, sitting up straight and saying that stories on office clothes — work wardrobes, she called them — were the bread and butter of Canadian fashion magazines.

"Work wardrobes, bread and butter — got it."

"So your father knows Campbell Cameron?" Marni said. A sudden change of tack. "Should I know your father?"

"Oh. No, I don't think so. His name's Angus. Angus McKinnon? He's in insurance. He knows Mr. Cameron from school, I think. And they're not big buddies or anything. Just acquaintances."

"I see. Well, I must say, you look different from what I expected."

"It's the clothes, right?" I gestured to my cheap dress. "I guess

I'm kind of lacking my own work wardrobe right now. But as soon as I get my first paycheque — "

The amused expression again. "I wasn't referring to your clothes."

"Oh." I looked at the floor. "I'm adopted. Is that what you meant?"

"Your looks make a nice change from WASPy types like Campbell Cameron."

I was still trying to come up with a reply to that one when she stood and held out her hand. "At any rate," she said, "welcome aboard."

On my first night back home from Paris that spring I spotted Brian Turnbull, my boyfriend Tom came over.

Like after every trip to Europe, I praised the food and the clothes and complained about the crowds and the delays. And like Tom did near the end of every documentary film he worked on, he announced that he was going to try for an assistant editor's job on a feature next, and this time he meant it, too. Our monologues out of the way, we smoked a couple of joints, consumed some Indian food I'd had delivered, and vegged in front of the TV, making derisive remarks about every show we flipped past. At eleven o'clock we got up from the couch, brushed our teeth, went to bed, and had sex — a satisfactory session, but not more.

Afterwards, I lay in bed and listened to Tom snore. I had no real reason to feel disappointed. None. Well, okay, maybe the sex could have been more exciting, considering I'd been away for a while, but after four years of this routine, what did I expect? Nothing fantastic.

Sex with Brian Turnbull *would* be fantastic, though. He would conduct grand seductions, for sure, with champagne and whirlpool baths in a sumptuous hotel suite, silk brocade draperies around the bed, dim lights, plush carpets.

I shook my head in the dark. What an image to harbour after only that one eye-lock in a crowded room. Still. I pictured Brian loosening his tie. There was something so sexy about a man in a suit, especially a man with Brian's body, Brian's suit.

Because Brian would wear a fabu-suit, Armani or Comme des Garçons, and he'd loosen his tie, and the woman with him would feel a surge of desire at the mere sight of his exposed Adam's apple. Then he'd say, in a to-die-for Australian accent . . . damn, what would he say? Oh, I don't know, something mannish but romantic, gruff but melting. Soft music would be playing, the glasses would be long-stemmed, so would the roses, and . . .

I drifted off, happy.

Chapter Two

By the time the *Panache* contingent hit New York a month later, I'd built my Brian dreams into epics, complete with full wardrobe, makeup, hair, and feature-length scripts. So I won't deny I was on the lookout for the man in the flesh as we made our way around the fall collections. Antenna extended way up for that V-build, that craggy profile, those eyes.

And I wasn't disappointed. Not only did I catch sight of his eyes — and the rest of him — all over the place, but he looked even better than I'd remembered. There was none of this, Oh no, he's shorter than I thought, or, What's with the double chin? action. No way. More like Dreamboat City all over again.

Yeah, I had a great time seeking him out in every venue, brushing past him accidentally once or twice or ten times.

But on the last day of showings, imagine my shock to see him moving through the crowd straight toward me in the mêlée at the New York Public Library, where I stood alone waiting for my assistant, Helen — also known as my right hand — to return from the washroom. He made eye contact from about fifteen feet away. Yes, he was looking at me. Eek.

He stopped in front of me and extended his hand. "Hello," he said, "I don't believe I've had the pleasure. I'm Brian Turnbull, of *Fashion Folio*, in Sydney."

"Hi. Rosemary McKinnon. *Panache*, Toronto." I crushed his fingers in my sweaty palm.

"I don't make it round the circuit as much as I used to," he said, "but when I do, I like to meet all the English-language press. To make contacts, exchange ideas, that sort of thing."

Struck speechless by the spectacle of life imitating dream-building, I fell back on my dog impression — panting, tongue hanging out.

"I've been taking a survey," he said. He smiled then, and at the sight of his dimples I actually started to drool. "So what trends are you calling for the season?" he said.

Huh? Was it my turn to talk? I scrambled for an answer but all I could get out was some incoherent mumbling that might have contained the word "menswear." Either that, or "dandies." Or maybe neither, I can't be sure.

The thing was, I couldn't believe it. He'd approached *me*. He wanted to meet *me*. He, the gorgeous BMOC, had seen me across the crowded room and thought, Hey! there's an English-language press person I haven't met. He'd taken one look, and figured —

Wait a minute.

I sucked in some drool. "But how'd you know I was English-language press when you saw me? How'd you know I wasn't from Portugal or Sweden?"

Or Asia.

A sharp look flashed across his face, replaced by a fresh smile. "I gambled. But I couldn't lose — at worst, I'd meet a beautiful woman."

Gong.

Man of my dreams or not, I knew bullshit when I heard it. Beautiful woman? Look around, buddy, if you want to see beautiful women — they're the ones on the runway.

He leaned toward me, placed a hand on my shoulder, and spoke into my ear, though there was no need, I'd heard him perfectly well until then. "I'm arranging a quiet dinner tonight, just a few people, in a private room at a Japanese restaurant in SoHo, wonderful country food, very informal. Won't you join us?"

And — I gotta say — that extra few inches made the difference. The zoom-in on his tanned neck against the bright white of his starched shirt collar, the quiet scent of dangerous cologne that drifted off his skin — it was all too much.

"I . . . I . . . I . . . I don't know, my schedule's so busy . . ."

Helen squeezed in behind me. "Forget it, the line-up's too long." She noticed Brian. "Sorry, I didn't see you there. Hi, I'm Helen Lam."

"Wow!" she said, when I'd introduced him. "The mogul? Neat!"

He repeated his dinner invitation. "Perhaps you can convince Rosemary?"

"Come on, Rosemary," she said. "The alternative is another meal with Marni."

Helen and I exchanged glances.

"Okay," I said to Brian. "I guess. I mean, thank you. We'd love to come."

We arranged the where and when, and watched him walk away. "Very cute," Helen said. "Think he's straight?"

"I think he's married."

And I didn't just think this, I *knew*. I'd looked him up since Paris, done some research. "But why did he ask us to dinner?" I said. "Spotted our talent from across the room?"

Helen grinned. "Maybe he just likes slanted beavers."

"Helen. Please."

Many people go through life without ever hearing of slanted beavers. Helen knows the phrase because she's second-generation Chinese and plugged-in. I know because of my background. Which I suppose I should mention. Not my favourite topic, to be sure, but it has this way of coming up. Straight out: I look Asian. Oriental, they used to say. Eurasian, technically, because my mother was Vietnamese, my father French, from France. Give people a minute to digest the old birth facts and the next question is usually, "So how'd you get a last name like McKinnon?"

It's tempting to lie at that point. Hell, it's tempting to lie *before* that point. But most of the time I break down and explain that the McKinnon name came from my adoptive parents. And when I'm feeling truly expansive, I give more detail — about how my parents adopted me, an infant orphan, through some old-boy diplomatic connection of my dad's. How they brought me over from Saigon, introduced me to their ten-year-old biological daughter Julie, and raised me the only way they knew how, in the Anglo-Canadian tradition.

A tradition which did not, I admit, encompass parental guidance on the slanted beaver topic.

No, I have my grade thirteen boyfriend to thank for that. He of the glorious curly red hair and freckles, and the lovely lean build formed by endless hours of cross-country running, a pursuit I mistook at the time to be indicative of inner depths.

It was one night when we were drunk or stoned, maybe both, and making out on the floor of my family room, that he paused for air between hickeys and mumbled, "All the guys are asking me what's it like to have sex with a slanted beaver."

Well, it took me a few seconds — the same amount of time it took to unzip his fly and reach inside his underwear — to understand what he was talking about. I only wish I could say that, once I got the gist, I broke up with him then and there.

But I didn't. I just dropped his dick like a hot bratwurst and acted indignant, and he apologized without really understanding why, I think, and our relationship lasted until the day, a few months later, when I finally figured out that all he'd been pondering during his cross-country jaunts was whether he should have a Big Mac or a Quarter-Pounder when he was through. As in: he was cute, but that was all. There *was* no more.

In the meantime, I did begin to wonder if my vagina was a different shape than other women's. But it wasn't as if I could discuss the topic with my mother or with my blue-eyed, blonde sister, and I didn't know any of the Asian kids at school well enough to ask them. Not that they would have known, either. Eventually, after close examination of a few women's health books, I discovered that all vaginas were the same and that whoever coined the slanted beaver term was an ignorant, racist pig.

Mind you, this was when I was still a kid, before I'd ever seen a personals ad run by a "White Man Seeking Oriental Woman" and felt like I should wash my hands after holding the newspaper. Or maybe spring for an eyelid operation, just to be sure I never came into contact with a guy like that.

So imagine this: there you are, surrounded by supermodels and mortal models, women who devote their lives to being beautiful. And a charming, successful, sexy-as-all-hell man is courting, of all people, you.

How can this be? you wonder, as he pours you another glass of wine and says you're fascinating and intelligent and attractive in a way those empty-headed goddesses can never be. Why me? you think, as his leg brushes against yours and you feel your libido flare up to scorch level from mere contact between your skirt and the wool of his trousers.

He takes you back to your hotel and kisses you in the elevator, and you twirl into your hotel room, where the light is rosy, the curtains are drawn, and there's Spanish guitar music throbbing in the air. Your clothes fall off, so do his, and he's got a great body — all hard pecs and biceps and a washboard stomach, and you're looking not bad yourself. Check this out — your breasts have inflated so much you could pass for a Victoria's Secret lingerie model, complete with cleavage enhanced by a new forest green lace bra (with matching panties).

He takes the chocolate mints off the pillow and slips them into your mouth. You close your eyes, rub your new thinner thighs together, and think, "This is going to be fantastic!"

He leans down and kisses your neck. You lift your chin, shut your eyes, and hear him say, "Oriental girls are such a turn-on."

No. It wouldn't be like that. Helen was wrong, had been joking.

Ten minutes before the limo was due to arrive, I stood in front of my hotel room vanity mirror and combed my hair. I Q-tipped away a smudge in my eye makeup and examined my reflection one last time. I wore a black turtleneck, black long skirt, boots, and a clunky necklace. I looked a little forbidding. But at least I didn't look like a bargirl out of *Miss Saigon*.

Inside the restaurant, I took a seat in the middle of the long table. Helen was at one end, with two of Brian's editors — one Australian, one British — whom we'd met in the limo on the way down. We were eight in total, all journalists I learned when the introductions were made.

The waitress took drink orders, and, though everyone was into the *sake*, I ordered a beer. Then Brian and the waitress started conversing in what sounded to my ignorant ear like pretty fluent Japanese, causing Helen to shoot me a mischievous eye. "Does anyone mind if I order for all of us?" Brian asked, and did so.

The guy sitting next to me was named Matthew, from *L.A.* magazine. "Did you hear what happened backstage at Isaac Mizrahi?" he said.

We chatted away until I noticed that the woman beside Brian had her hand on his arm and was murmuring in his ear. Her name was Anna, I recalled, and she worked for a South American newspaper chain, which made her Spanish-language press, though her English was flawless. She passed the beautiful woman test anyway, with her short fair hair in a great cut, her straight nose, her long neck. Bony shoulders and hillocks of flesh overflowing her wine-coloured velvet bustier completed the picture — my basic worst nightmare.

Brian laughed at something she'd said, then turned and caught me looking sick across from him. I cleared my face and asked him to pass me the sushi.

Dishes of food were arriving every minute now. "Almost too beautiful to eat, isn't it?" Anna said in her British accent.

I disagreed. The hot starchy stuff was calling me — bowls of brown rice with a fragrant Japanese herb mixed in, golden tempura slices of potato and sweet potato, and a big tureen of long thin noodles coiled in a steaming broth.

Brian was serving the noodle soup into smaller bowls. "Who would like some ramen?"

"I would, I would!" I said, though I noticed both Anna and Matthew refused any.

I pulled the small bowl close, picked up several strands of noodles with my chopsticks, and brought them to my mouth. I drew in the first few inches of noodles and started chewing. So far, so good — both taste and texture were satisfying. Soothing, even. I sucked in another wad, looked down, and realized that these noodles were long, I mean, *really* long, and what had started out as a few strands had become a big clump between my lips. And there was no conceivable way of dealing with the clump unless I got into major slurping or did that biting-off thing which I've always detested because it looks as if you're spitting food back into your plate — a pretty disgusting sight. Especially if the person with the best view would be Brian, who — noodle-less himself — picked this moment to say, "How's the ramen, Rosemary?"

I nodded in reply — not a smart move, because the nodding action caused some drops of soup to fly onto the tablecloth. So I held my head very still and pulled noodles up to my mouth in tiny increments. But when my wild-eyed glance around caught an expression of amused condescension on Anna's face, I abandoned all attempts at decorum and hoovered in the rest of the mouthful in one loud slurp, a manoeuvre which splattered liquid clear across the table and onto Brian's shirt.

"God, I'm so sorry. Your shirt — forgive me." I covered my face with my hands. "Can't take me anywhere."

"Don't worry," Brian said. "Slurping's the proper way to eat soup in Japan, you know."

I looked out from between my fingers and saw Brian stand up. He leaned over the table and dabbed at my necklace and sweater with his napkin.

When he'd sat down again, Anna said, "*Are* you Japanese, Rosemary?"

I felt more than saw Helen's head move forward. "No." I looked Anna straight in her deep-lidded eyes. "Are you?"

An uncertain little laugh. "No."

Matthew, at my side. "Rosemary, some sea urchin?"

"Oh. No thanks." The substance he was offering looked pretty gag-inducing, texture-wise, and I needed to take a rest from eating anything right then.

"So, Brian," Matthew said. "Have you ever eaten live shrimp at a sushi bar? That wriggling sensation in your throat as they go down? That's some kick, isn't it?" He went on in this vein while I sat there and breathed. In a few minutes, I was able to pick up some rice and get it down without choking, force out a few smiles and chuckles at the right places in the conversation.

After we'd drunk green tea and Brian had taken care of the bill without its appearing at the table, Anna suggested we all go out to a club. Or rather, she put her elbows on the table, pressed her breasts together, and said, mainly to Brian, "Who feels like dancing?"

Maybe it was the *sake*, but everyone was wild about this idea, Helen included.

Brian said, "What about you, Rosemary? You game?"

I saw a crowded room, heavy drug consumption in the washroom, women in Versace bondage dresses writhing on the dance floor. In the middle of this scene, there I was, hot and sweaty in my black wools, sitting beside Helen, yelling the occasional comment in her ear — and waiting in vain for my crush-object to ask me to dance.

I looked at Brian's handsome face. Who was I kidding? "I think I'll make it an early night, thanks."

Everyone stood up and headed for the washroom or the coat check. Amid the hubbub, Brian said, "Shall I see you back to the hotel, then?"

"No, no," I said, "you go on. I'll grab a cab."

But a few minutes later I was outside on the curb, and he was standing there with me waving goodbye to the others, who had squeezed into one car and were driving away, ha-haing and hoo-hoo-ing. Anna blew a kiss to Brian out the window. "We'll be waiting!" she called.

He opened the back door of the remaining limo for me. "Hop in. It won't take a minute to run you uptown."

For a few blocks we rode along in the velveteen silence of the back seat. I looked straight ahead and tried to think of a good open-ing line. Something like, What about those Knicks? Except maybe he wouldn't know what I was talking about. Plus *I* wouldn't know what I was talking about. I was still working on it when I realized he was staring at my profile, had been for a few minutes now.

The car splashed through some puddles. I glanced out at the shiny wet road and up at the streetlights on Eighth Avenue and had just concluded, based on my limited knowledge of lighting, that this particular combination of factors was not the most flattering, was probably magnifying the pores in my chin and enlarging my nos-tril holes, both of which have a tendency to be less than delicate anyway, when he said, "You have such an intriguing face."

Uh-oh.

He tried again. "With a name like McKinnon, your father's a Scot?"

I considered which of my arsenal of answers to that question I should let fire, but I came up empty. "It's kind of a long story."

He spoke softly. "I'd like to hear it."

"My birth father was French and my birth mother Vietnamese. My adoptive parents are Scottish. And English. It's complicated."

"Well, whoever your parents were, they certainly produced a beautiful combination." He reached up and tucked my hair behind my left ear. "Are you close to your family?"

I shook the hair free. "Fairly. I call my mother a lot, my sister and I are friendly . . . and my dad and I sail together in the summer."

"Where?"

"In Toronto. On Lake Ontario. He has a small centreboard boat. We go out for the evening races the odd time when the weather's good." *Ask him something.* "What about you? See much of your relatives?"

"No. My mother's dead. And my father and I don't get on. He doesn't understand why I don't do something manly, work with my hands, like he did, building houses. An honest profession, he says, not like me, larking about with a bunch of faggots, worrying about women's clothes."

Ah . . . er . . . that is . . . I . . . "Why *did* you go into the business?"

"To be around good-looking women, of course." He started a big grin, then read my face and toned it down. "No, truly, I started out as an art director for a women's magazine, developed a bit of a reputation, went on from there." I waited to hear the rest of the story, but he leaned over me, pressed the button to roll down my window, and said, "I believe this is your hotel."

The limo rolled to a stop. I opened the car door and bolted out before the driver had a chance to walk around. "Bye," I called into the back seat. "Thanks again for dinner and for the lift."

Brian stepped out and stood on the street. "It's been lovely," he said. "We'll have to do it again sometime."

I said Sure, sounds great, mumbled goodbye, and hurried up the sidewalk carpet toward the hotel entrance. But when I heard the car door close behind me with a final thud, I ran back and knocked on the window.

"Listen," I said, when he'd powered it down, "if you're ever in Toronto, in the summer, I'll take you sailing. On a clear night, with a good wind, a friendly race — maybe it's a stupid idea. Never mind. Anyway. Goodnight."

I ran into the hotel and up to my room. "Good one, Rosemary," I said to myself as I went. "Very cool. The epitome of cool, in fact. Jesus."

In the room, I took off my clothes, pulled on a T-shirt, piled up some pillows on the bed against the headboard, sat down, turned on the TV, turned it off, jumped up, paced, brushed my teeth, swore, thought about punching the wall. And was startled as hell when the bedside fax machine rang. I watched the fax come through and read the neat handwriting — art director handwriting.

> *My dear Rosemary,*
> *Your invitation to sail was the best I've received in a long while. I look forward to taking you up on it.*
>
> *Regards,*
> *Brian*

He'd faxed me from the car.

I called room service to send up a cappuccino and started working on some serious dream-building.

At breakfast the next day in the hotel, a wasted Helen reported that Anna had draped herself all over Brian at the dance club.

"He kept her at arm's length, though, no matter how many times she pressed those fake tits against him or let her hand trail across his lap."

Marni sat down at our table. "Whose hand across whose lap?"

Helen turned her baggy eyes toward Marni's crisp makeup job. "Talking about our night on the town with Brian Turnbull."

Marni flared her nostrils. "I can imagine."

"He seems pleasant enough," I said. "Why don't you like him?"

"He's a notorious womanizer. Such a bore."

Helen yawned. "Well, he wasn't hitting up on anyone last night. Unless he put a move on Rosemary when he drove her back to the hotel. Did he? Come on, Rosemary, you can tell us."

I thought of Brian's fax smouldering in my bag. "Are you kidding? It was strictly shop talk." I picked up my coffee cup and took a swig, but I could feel Marni's eyes on me. "What?" I said to her.

"So, Marni," Helen said, "you're not going to believe who I saw snorting coke in the washroom at this dance club last night."

Marni bit, Helen started telling her anecdote, and I remembered, not for the first time, to be grateful for Helen.

Chapter Three

It had only been about a year and a half before that New York trip when Marni had said to me, late one afternoon, "By the way, someone's been hired to be your new assistant fashion editor."

"I guess it's too much to ask that I have some say in hiring my own staff?"

"Maybe you already know this person. She's fresh out of the Ryerson fashion program, but she was in high school with Campbell Cameron's youngest daughter. Isn't your family also friends with his?"

"Unfair. I've advanced to my current illustrious position *despite* my father being acquainted with Mr. Cameron."

Marni fished a résumé out a pile of paper on her desk. "Her name is . . . let's see . . . Helen. Helen Lam. She starts in three weeks. Look after it."

Did I have a choice? No. So there I was one morning in the *Panache* lobby, welcoming aboard a petite but leggy person with short dark hair streaked white, wearing fifties-style eyeglasses and a dress I would later realize was two seasons ahead of its time.

I toured her around the offices, spent the requisite hour going over first-day details, and started doling out her assignments: make these phone calls, file these items, read and memorize the last twelve issues of *Panache*. "Oh, and we'll need ten copies of this proposal for the meeting on Wednesday." I handed her a document. "Distribute the copies to the editorial committee, keep one for yourself, read it over. You can attend the meeting, too, see how decisions get made around here. Just don't speak."

I looked up and saw an unhappy face. "Don't speak at the meeting, I mean."

"You're asking me to make photocopies?"

"Yeah. Either get the secretary to do it, or do it yourself. As long as they're done on time."

"I see."

"Is there a problem?"

"No. No problem. Other than that I haven't been trained for go-fer work. But that's okay. I'll figure it out." She stuck her pen behind her ear and started gathering up her stuff. "How long were you assistant again, before you got promoted?"

"Three years."

She sighed. "That long? Maybe I should have taken that retail job after all."

I said nothing, mainly because I didn't know how to respond to such cheek.

"But if you want photocopies, I'll make photocopies."

Count to five and breathe. "Good. Any other questions?"

"Well, yeah. I did have one. When they told me I'd be working with you, I never knew you were Oriental. From your name, I mean. But you're half-something, right? Half-what?"

I looked at her. A dirty look.

"Korean?" she said. "Japanese?"

I wanted to say, Half-pissed-off, but I'm occasionally a prisoner of my polite upbringing. So I said, "Vietnamese."

"Yeah? Vietnamese? But you're not a boat person, right? Were you born here?"

"No. It's a long story, and I don't particularly — "

"Okay, never mind. I was just wondering. But if you're touchy about it, hey."

She turned and walked out, and I laid my head down on the desk.

It could only get better after that, Helen and me. And it did, largely because underneath the attitude, she was quick and hard-working and reliable.

Though it was probably a mistake to send her upstairs that one time — way too early in her tenure — to get Campbell Cameron's approval on the models for a swimsuit story. As soon as she walked into my office, I knew I'd blown it. She sank down in a chair and made a gagging motion with her finger inside her mouth.

"He went for the D-cup," I said. Not a question.

"It's *how* he did it. He leered. He actually leered at every head sheet. I felt like I was watching someone read a skin magazine."

Welcome to the real world. "At least we can finish setting up the shoot now. That's worth celebrating. How about lunch? On my expense account. Feel like pasta?"

"Actually, I was going to ask you for dim sum today. It's Chinese New Year."

Who would have thought? "Sure," I said, "Lead the way."

We sat in a crowded room full of mostly Asian people, sipped our Chinese tea, and waited for the carts to come by. "Do you eat dim sum often?" I asked.

"Hardly ever. I usually get lunch from that Italian place across the road from the office. I'm totally into the bruschetta."

A waitress had wheeled up our first trolley. She lifted the lid off the top bamboo steamer on the stack and said something to me in Chinese. I looked at a mystery substance, then at Helen. "No thanks," we both said. The waitress moved on.

"What *was* that, do you think?" I said.

"Tripe, maybe?"

A young man whom I'd noticed walking across the room from another table stopped behind Helen and tapped her on the shoulder. "Hi, Helen. How are you? *Gong hay fat choy.*"

"Happy New Year," Helen said, and introduced him to me as David Chen, a friend of her family. I noted his gelled hair and expensive casual clothes, and listened while he and Helen carried on a somewhat forced conversation about mutual acquaintances, during which I said yes to a waitress offering shrimp dumplings and no to one bearing chicken feet.

The David guy was pulling out a chair — to join us? — when

Helen interrupted whatever he was saying. "You'll have to excuse us, David. Rosemary and I are having a business lunch here. We have a lot to cover. Give my best to your parents. Bye."

"Okay," I said when he was out of earshot. "What was the story there?"

Helen picked up a dumpling with her chopsticks. "You wouldn't understand."

"Try me."

"It's my parents. They've been trying to set me up with him. You know — a nice Chinese boy."

"He seemed okay. Kind of cute. Nice clothes. Does he work?"

"He's a medical student."

"Oh. I see."

"Look. There's nothing wrong with the guy — I just don't happen to find him attractive or interesting. And despite what my parents think, we have nothing in common. He's very traditional. The only good thing about it is, he doesn't like me much, either."

"Why not?"

"He wants an old-fashioned Chinese girl. He'll probably end up going to China and importing a nice servile bride."

"And where does that leave you?"

"Giving up on romance, basically. Considering that the Chinese guys I know are so uncool, and the white men I meet are either unavailable or dirty old men like Campbell Cameron."

"Listen. About Campbell. I guess I should say something."

"Go ahead."

"He has no redeeming qualities."

Helen laughed.

"The trick," I said, "is to avoid all contact. And hope we can stick it out until he retires."

"How old is he?"

"Fifty-five?"

"You don't seriously expect to still be at *Panache* in ten years, do you?"

"Come on, Helen. Think positive. Look ahead. We'll work our way up, topple the old regime, change the world."

"Yeah, right," she said, "sure thing."

We lifted our teacups and drank to it anyway.

Back at the office after lunch, we ran into Campbell Cameron in the corridor outside my office. Standing there clutching an 8x10 of Natasha, the buxom sixteen-year-old he'd selected for the swimsuit story.

"Oh, there you are, sweetheart," he said to Helen. "You left this in my office. And much as I'd like to get it blown up to life-size for my office wall, I thought I should return it." He chuckled.

We gave him back our best stone faces.

He looked at me, then at Helen. "You know, I'm just off to a meeting upstairs with little Paul Yamaguchi." He placed a hand on Helen's shoulder. "Do you know him, dear?"

No, she didn't.

"Oh, I thought you might. He's an interior designer. He's been hired to redo the executive offices for all of MacKenzie Communications." He pointed at me now. "You know Paul, don't you, ahh . . ."

"Rosemary. Yeah, I know Paul. We've featured his retail work in the magazine a few times."

"Well, this design stuff's all Greek to me. I told the girl co-ordinating the project I don't care what he does as long as I can still wear my shoes in the office!" He nudged Helen and winked. "See you girls later."

I looked at Helen. She looked at me. And I knew I didn't need to tell her that Paul Yamaguchi was a six-foot-tall, third-generation Japanese-Canadian whose current design inspiration was southern France.

"Could you believe that comment?" I said.

"Which one?"

That was it. That's what she said. She didn't say, "What comment?" or "You're awfully sensitive," or "Gee, that's some big chip on your shoulder."

I liked that.

Chapter Four

On Turnbull Publications, Inc., letterhead, the fax read:

To: R. McKinnon, Fashion Editor, Panache
From: Mr. Brian Turnbull

Will be in Toronto first week of July.
Does sailing invitation still stand?
Reply to New York office.
Regards.

I read it over four times, a fifth. Could this really be happening? Hours of dream-building aside, I'd never thought anything would come of my impulsive invitation to take Brian sailing or of his businesslike fax to my hotel room.

Okay, yes, I had broken up with my boyfriend Tom when I'd returned home from New York that time after the Japanese dinner. But not because I was seriously hoping to have an affair with a married mogul. More due to the appalling differences between the way things were and the way I dreamed they could be.

I reread the fax, turned on my computer, started composing a reply, and noticed that my body had locked into megacrush mode: my heart thumped, I wheezed, and beads of sweat were forming in all the usual places.

It looked like I was going sailing.

By the time Brian called me in the afternoon of the appointed day, I'd checked the weather once an hour since six that morning, so I was fully acquainted with the forecast. It was unseasonably cold, overcast, wind blowing 35 m.p.h., gusts to 50, with an 80% chance of precipitation by nightfall. Not the kind of conditions for a friendly sail between virtual strangers.

"So are we on?" Brian said.

My body reacted to the sound of his voice with a rush that made me grip my desktop. "Uh, I'm afraid the weather doesn't look too great . . ."

"Come now," he said, confirming what I'd suspected — that his ruddy complexion had been earned on the water. And that his interest was in sailing, not in me. "I'm looking out my hotel window at the bay right now and conditions look glorious. Now, what kind of boat are we sailing?"

"A Flying Dutchman."

"Why, you darling girl! Where do we meet?"

I waited on a wooden bench at quayside. I eyed the whitecaps on the grey water and shivered, despite my jeans and sweater. I checked my watch every thirty seconds, watched the sidewalk for his approach, and used my spare time to quell the image that crowded my mind: his hotel suite, somewhere close by.

I took a minute to feel bad about hiding this rendezvous from Helen. She'd come by my desk at 5:15 and found me changed into my sailing clothes, carefully lining my lips. "Heavy date?" she'd asked.

I kept my eyes on the compact mirror I held. "Date? You kidding? What *is* dating, anyway?"

"Okay, give. Who is he?"

"My dad. We're going sailing."

"Your dad rates lip pencil and" — she leaned forward and examined my face — "foundation?"

I peered into the mirror. "Shit, does it show? Can you really tell?"

"Don't worry. Only a pro would spot it."

"Oh, great." I picked up a tissue from the box on my desk and started dabbing.

Helen didn't move. "Rosemary, believe me, your dad will never know, or care."

"Shouldn't you be getting home now, Helen? Wouldn't want anyone saying we work you too hard."

"Fine. I get the message. Say hi to your 'dad' for me."

Nice to know this romance that wasn't a romance was making me be mean to my best work friend. Another excellent reason not to hope for anything developing with Brian. Not that any number of solid reasons could have kept me from the dock that night.

He arrived punctually at 5:59. He wore leather deck shoes, faded jeans, and a blue polo shirt, its collar turned up under a sweater of the same colour. Over an arm he had flung a yellow storm jacket.

"Hi," I said. "The tender should be along to take us across to the yacht club in a few minutes."

He squinted at the sky. "Wonderful weather!" He looked down at me. "You feeling all right?" He slid his cool hand along my hot cheek and around the back of my neck.

He was touching me. "Uh, I guess I'm just stressed out from work."

"What's stressing you at work?"

"Oh, you know, the usual. I'm sure every magazine's the same."

He studied my face and spoke gently. "Tell me about yours."

I checked his expression to see if he was being polite and was surprised to see what looked like genuine concern there. *Quick. Think of something.* I racked my brain and surprised myself with my answer. "Oh, probably everyone who's ever worked anywhere has ideas of how they'd do things differently if they were running the place."

"And what would you change?"

I took a deep breath and launched into a speech about how, if I ruled the world, there'd be fewer meetings, more E-mail, and more experimentation. With something as simple as using non-white models or running a beauty story that did more than tout our advertisers' new products. I talked about playing against type, about reversing expectations.

"And who's the obstacle to change in your case?" Brian said. "Your publisher, your editor?"

"The publisher, mostly. He's, like, brother, from another era. Calling women girls and thinking business is about having drinks at the club."

"And Marni Cohen?"

"Marni's okay. She's kind of prickly, but she's smart. And she's been good to me. It was probably her who first got me thinking that one day we could do something different, show them all."

"Show who all?"

"Sexist old-style male publishing magnates, mostly." I laughed. "Are you one of those?"

He smiled. "Definitely."

I smiled back, but I decided I'd better change the subject, and fast. What had come over me? I sounded like an earnest young journalism graduate, full of sappy ideals. I stood up. "Here's the tender." We moved toward the queue forming on the dock. "Listen, about tonight, I wanted to ask — how much sailing have you done exactly?"

"Some. I quite like a Flying Dutchman, though — I competed internationally in the Flying Dutchman a few years back." A rueful smile. "More than a few years ago. Almost twenty."

"You sailed in world championships?" Gulp. "Tell you what — I'll crew, and you take the helm."

"No, no, I wouldn't presume. It's your boat, your lake, you be in charge."

The line-up started to move forward. "No, really," I said. "I'd like you to be the skipper tonight. Okay?"

But I didn't catch his answer because my hair started flying around in the wind and whipped me right in the eye, hard, bringing tears. I dug into my bag, found a covered elastic, and quickly tied my hair into a loose braid. "Okay?" I said. "You'll sail?"

Brian offered me his arm for balance as I stepped aboard the tender. "It would be my pleasure," he said.

Over on the island side, we zipped ourselves into our wetsuits, rigged the boat, lowered it into the water, and caught a stiff breeze in the lagoon that carried us out halfway to where the race course had been laid out in the bay.

We sailed back and forth a bit, Brian getting a feel for the boat, for the wind. I explained how the local race committee ran the races, what timing signals they used, showed him the first upwind mark. I buckled the trapeze harness around my chest, fastened the strap between my legs, and tested its tension against the mast. On the first leg of the race, the upwind leg, we'd both hang out over the side of the boat — me standing, suspended on the trapeze, he hiking from his perch on the gunwale — and use our combined weight to keep us level.

In the minutes before the race, we sat a few yards back from the start, luffing in irons and waiting for the gun. During the countdown, the boats behind the line jostled for the upwind position. Next to us, an arm's length away on our starboard side, also in a Flying Dutchman, sat Charlie Barrett and Terry McNally, two golden-boy hotshots I'd known since I was a kid.

"Hey, Rosemary!" Charlie called out after the one-minute warning gun had been fired. I glanced at him and nodded. He'd called me slant-eyed once when I was ten and I'd never forgotten it.

"What's that between your legs, Rosemary?" he said. He meant the trapeze harness. Great sense of humour, huh. His friend Terry laughed.

Brian looked at me sideways. I checked my watch: ten seconds.

I whispered the count to Brian, waited five, then yelled out,

"Charlie, watch out! You're over the line!" and pulled with all my strength on the jib sheet, while Brian headed us out of irons and across the start in perfect sync with the gun. We were first across the line, but Charlie and Terry floundered two boat-lengths behind. Even with the wind blowing toward them, I could hear the swearing.

Brian headed the boat closer in to the wind. I scrambled up onto the gunwale and leaned out backwards over the rushing water. From this position, I controlled the jib sheet, he the tiller. He shouted commands, not unkindly but urgently. Get out on that trapeze. Now down. Pull the jib in. Harder! Wait, ease up. And I obeyed, followed his lead.

We stayed ahead through the first leg. When we'd rounded the buoy, I looked back and saw we had a good lead on the closest boat, though Charlie and Terry were right behind it in third.

The second leg was a reach, the wind coming across our beam. I spent less time on the trapeze and more sitting on the gunwale.

"You all right?" Brian said after a while. I nodded and ungritted my teeth. I hadn't felt tension like this in a race since I'd been a teenager. Race nights with my dad were always on sunlit evenings in moderate winds, sailing with friends.

Brian looked back, so did I, and we saw that Charlie had taken second place, though he was still a good distance behind us. Brian slid up next to me and spoke quietly. "After we jibe around the next mark, I want you to throw the spinnaker forward of the forestay, collect the spinnaker sheets, then come back to the stern. Got it?"

"We can't fly the spinnaker in this wind."

"Let's see if we can do a little planing. Prepare to jibe."

The boom flew across the boat, and I stepped over with it. Planing? Was he crazy? Planing was wild speed sailing that happened when a strong wind — gale-force, for instance — pushed you from behind, very fast. If you threw all your weight to the back of the boat to keep it flat, and set your sails right, you could do it. So the theory went. Not something I'd actually experienced.

"Spinnaker!" Brian yelled.

I threw the spinnaker forward. Brian stood, stuck the tiller between his legs, adjusted the mainsail, and grabbed hold of the spinnaker halyard. I edged back, took hold of the spinnaker sheets, and waited. Brian looked behind us, watching the wind blow across the water. "Here we go," he said, and hoisted the spinnaker. "Here we fucking well go."

We were speeding along quickly enough until then, but when the spinnaker rose to its full height, a big gust puffed it out and we shot forward, skimming the tops of the waves. I screamed a rollercoaster-ride scream and snuck a peek at Brian, who sat there, quiet, eyes sparkling, a rabid grin on his face.

I could have stared at him forever, except the elastic holding my braid in place must have worked itself loose, because my hair suddenly started flying all over again. I squinted, fearing another whiplash in the eye. Until Brian, in one quick movement, grabbed my hair, twisted it into a tail, and tucked it inside my collar. And let his hand linger there a second longer than necessary.

Nah. I must have imagined it. Why would he stroke my hair in the middle of a race? I thanked him, and risked a glance back at Charlie's boat, half a leg behind. "I think we're going to win."

"Did you ever doubt it?"

We won the second race, too, and then the committee boat called it a night, for which I was glad. Enough already with the great outdoors.

We sailed back in, unrigged the boat, grabbed some takeout coffees from the clubhouse, and ran to catch the tender back to the city. Inside the warm cabin, I sat beside Brian, ears buzzing, and didn't feel much of anything. The combination of a bad sleep the night before, suffering a state of anticipation all day, and tense races in heavy weather had added up to turn me into a bag of bones with tangled hair, wet clothes, and makeup all wiped off. Not the most enticing figure, to be sure, though Brian looked ready to acquire a few media conglomerates before bedtime — face glowing, hair curling in the mist. I sat back and admired his beauty, but my loins did not stir. My skin was too cold and clammy and puckered to respond, even to him.

We stepped onto the dock on the city side. The forecast rain had begun — heavy, cold, blown by wind. We ducked inside a transit shelter on the sidewalk. "So," I said, "great sailing. Thanks for coming. I'll have to import you for the next regatta. And, well, goodnight."

He placed his hand under my chin and gazed into my sunken eyes. "I can't convince you to come out for a late supper?"

The rain beat against the glass of the shelter, and I saw the structure sway in the wind. "I'd love to, but I'm afraid I'd either fall asleep or throw up on the table. Or do both. But I can drive you to your hotel, because of the rain, I mean. I'm parked right across the street."

"Thanks. I'll walk. I don't get out in the weather enough."

He took hold of me by the shoulders. I hung limp in his arms. He gave me a quick kiss on the cheek. "The evening was marvellous," he said. "Thank you. I'm flying out early tomorrow, but I'll be in touch."

He charged off, face upturned to the rain like some sort of Nature Man. I shivered, ran to my car, started it, and pulled out of the parking lot. I peered out the blurry windshield, blinked to clear away the triple images of headlights reflected in the puddles on the road, and resolved to forget all about him.

Chapter Five

I stood up from the visitor's chair in Marni's office, ready to go.

"Oh, Rosemary," she said, "one more thing. You'll never guess who's coming to Europe with us in September."

"Is it Helen? She'd love to go."

"No, sorry."

"Who then?"

"Carolyn Whiting."

I sat down. "You're kidding."

"Can you believe it? An art director coming to the collections? Campbell's idea." A pause. "The imbecile."

"This wouldn't have anything to do with Carolyn pressing that bosom of hers against him at the anniversary party, would it?"

Panache's annual summer party had been held a few weeks before. One of those employee-only deals — no dates allowed — during cocktail hour at a flavour-of-the-month restaurant downtown.

Picture it: sales reps getting drunk, flirting going on between bad-news people combinations, and me, sitting on a bar stool nursing my Perrier and listening to Marni drone on.

Marni was telling a story about her recent vacation to Tuscany which I'd already heard, but it had good food details and was giving me some ideas about what I might whip up for dinner if I ever got out of there. So I nodded in all the right places, pictured a steaming plate of pasta tossed with white beans, olive oil, fresh tomato chunks and shaved Reggiano, and watched Carolyn Whiting enter the room and look around for suitable prospects.

Though Carolyn is my age, and short — maybe five-two — she's always looked older than me. Not in a matronly way, more like maybe I dress too young.

For example, that night I was wearing a short black pleated skirt, a white T-shirt, and high-cut Chuck Taylors with hockey socks —

fairly casual, even for me, but I'd come straight from a photo shoot in a ravine, where I'd spent the afternoon being eaten by mosquitoes.

So had Carolyn come from the shoot, but in her linen shift, tanned bare legs, low-heeled flat sandals, she looked more put-together, more sophisticated. And more sexy. The dress she wore was neither low-cut nor tight, but there was something about the way she carried herself.

I watched her approach a small group of people, make a motion like she was trying to swim through them, tilt her head, then say something which made everyone laugh. Three times I watched her do a variation on this theme, and I marvelled at how each time she managed to grab a man's arm, or whisper in a man's ear.

Marni finished up her story.

"I think I might head off," I said. Only I spoke too soon after she'd stopped, as if I'd been waiting impatiently to get a word in. Which I had.

She gave me a dirty look. "So go."

Carolyn materialized at Marni's side. "You two are standing over here looking awfully serious. Smile!"

Carolyn had already suggested I smile a few times that day out in the ravine, and I'd found her suggestions a little annoying. "How're your mosquito bites?" I asked her. I could only hope they were numerous and itchy.

"I don't think I got any. I must have the wrong blood type."

Marni, to Carolyn. "The shoot went well?"

"We had the most marvellous light. Didn't we, Rosemary?"

I said Yeah through an enormous nostril-flaring yawn, closed my mouth, and then said, "Oh, hi, Mr. Cameron," for there he was, the Big Cheese, beside me, giving each of us the once-over and letting his eyes linger on Carolyn's chest.

"You folks having a good time?" He put his arm around Carolyn and beamed at Marni and me.

Carolyn turned in his embrace, looked up at him, and jerked off his tie. "Wonderful party, Cam."

I woke up. Cam? She called the guy I still addressed as Mr. Cameron, even after all these years, Cam? And what was with the neckwear intimacy?

"I'm glad you girls are enjoying yourselves," said "Cam." Marni and I made fake enjoyment noises and I tried not to stare at his age-spotted fingers leaving indentations in the fair skin of Carolyn's forearm.

"It's such a lovely party!" Carolyn said. "Everything's so lavish."

I looked around, hard-pressed to agree. The tired-looking canapés had been of the standard mini-quiche, imitation-crab variety, and there hadn't been that many, I'd noticed.

Carolyn was saying, "And it's especially delightful to be here after spending all day in the woods struggling with winter coats."

"You'd look great in a mink yourself, my dear," Campbell said, and he looked down at her with great longing. Probably picturing her naked beneath a fur, the lech.

Behind their backs, I caught Marni's eye and tried rolling mine, but she wouldn't play.

I turned back to the sideshow and watched Campbell squeeze Carolyn closer, so her body pressed against his for a moment. She could have pulled away, but I distinctly saw her relax her pillowy chest into the expanse of hand-tailored English shirtfront that was Campbell's one claim to sartorial grandeur.

"Ouch!" Carolyn said, in a playful tone, and stepped back. "I think maybe I did get bitten today!" And she lifted the neckline of her dress and looked inside her cleavage for swellings.

Before Campbell could volunteer to rub on some calamine lotion, I stood up quickly and said my goodbyes. It was definitely time to go home.

Marni said, "Only five months to retirement and he pulls a stunt like this."

"Just tell me he's not coming to Europe, too."

"He isn't. Just her. He feels she needs to experience the prêt-à-porter first-hand. Grasp the zeitgeist."

"And whatever else will get her ahead."

Marni waved a hand. "Now you know."

I left her office. So much for my secret plan to get horizontal with Brian Turnbull in Europe. Bad enough Marni would be around, but Carolyn, too? I was history. Or, considering what my relationship with Brian consisted of so far, make that prehistory.

I hadn't heard from Brian since that night on the water in July, and I'd told myself a few times, over solitary bowls of ice cream (small, sprinkled with pecans), or popcorn (big, popped in extra virgin olive oil), that it was time to kick him out of my mind, and out of my dreams, once and for all.

Which doesn't explain why my travel preparations included a full-scale body wax, one of my least favourite things to do. No, Europe in October is not a venue where thigh- or armpit-baring is generally called for in the line of fashion editor duty. And your legs don't get too much exposure either. Unless you're planning on sharing a bed with a person you have the feeling would not exactly be turned on by stubble anywhere, or, more specifically, by the sight of pubic hair growing halfway down the insides of your (or in this case, my) thighs.

So I made an appointment at a snooty salon I'd once overheard Carolyn recommend, with someone named Elsa, for eight o'clock one morning. Not a time I usually reserve for anything other than mainlining coffee, but I knew if I arranged it for any later in the day I'd end up cancelling, just to avoid the whole process.

Because there's something about being waxed that is too weird to allow much premeditation, and I don't mean the pain. That's nothing to the strain of keeping up the small talk, as in, "You went on a cruise? Really? How was the food?" while some strange woman's fingers are sliding under the edge of your underpants, giving you a wedgie when she pulls up the elasticized leg at an alarming angle and asks, "How high do you want it?"

So eight a.m. it is, and there I am, bleary-eyed and caffeine-deprived, shoulders hunched, lying on one of those paper-covered beauty salon loungers in my underwear and bra, when Elsa enters the room and says Hello, how are you? in what sounds like a Teutonic accent. "Please lie down," she says next. "We do bikini first." She hooks the side of my underpants with her pinky and pulls up hard. "How high?"

"Oh, nothing extreme, just there is fine. Whatever."

Silence follows while she turns her back and readies her equipment, and I dare to hope that Elsa is the quiet type.

She reappears at my side, presses her abdomen into my hip, and leans over me. I arrange my legs obligingly into stork position, and she starts stroking the old bikini area with baby powder. Soft, soothing powder. Right on this very sensitive part of my thigh, where it joins the trunk of the body, which makes it not even technically a thigh anymore — we're verging on genitalia here.

And I'm lying there trying to convince myself that the sensation of her fingertips touching what is basically the border of a major erogenous zone has not registered in the part of my brain reserved for good sex vibes. A part not accustomed to this rather kinky scenario — me dressed in lingerie (if you can call a plain white bra and red cotton underpants lingerie), spread-eagled under the bright fluorescent lights, Elsa in a authoritarian white coat, both of our bodies tensed as she applies hot wax to my inner thigh with a wooden tongue depressor.

Elsa has said nothing further, so the rip of the waxing cloth pulling out the little hairs by the roots is the only sound in the room for a while.

Rip. Fingertips pushed against the raw waxed skin to ease the pain. Warm wax spread on the next section of thigh. Soft cloth pressed down on the wax. Pause. Rip. The rhythm's almost relaxing. I start thinking over what I have to do today, start looking forward to the toasted foccacia bagel and takeout latte I'll pick up after this at the bagel place next door.

Elsa's fingers smooth a cool creme on the waxed area. "Finished bikini. We do underarm now, yes?" she says.

I lie back, my arms raised above my head. The powder smells sweet. I close my eyes and see myself striding through Heathrow airport. My clothes are wrinkle-free, skin dewy, lipstick fresh. I've ditched Marni and Carolyn somewhere — good move, because look who's down the hallway, waving at me. He must have just arrived, too. What a coincidence! He waits until I draw closer, then falls into step beside me. "Hello," Brian says, or more like, "Hallo," and then —

Somewhere very close, I hear a door open and shut, and voices. I open my eyes and see that the partitions in the waxing room don't reach all the way to the ceiling.

"Now let's take a look at that broken nail," a loud voice says. "Oh, it's not too bad. I'll file it down, glue a new one over. Just take a minute." Sound of a stool being dragged across the tile floor. "So tell me, how've you been? Surviving the cold? Do you ski?" Obviously not all the aestheticians here go for Elsa's taciturn approach.

Elsa applies the last bit of creme to my armpits and asks me to bend one leg. She applies a strip of wax down my shin. Next door, I hear snatches of conversation above the intermittent hum of some sort of motorized nail tool. I strain to hear better because there's something familiar about the customer's voice.

"And how's work?" says the manicurist. The drone of the buffer or whatever it is stops, leaving a sudden quiet.

"Oh, work's fine," says a voice clearly, "for now."

I sit up. That's Carolyn's voice.

Elsa places her hands on my shoulders. "Lie down," she says. I do, and listen harder.

"I've been at the same place for five years now," says Carolyn, "but it's time to move on to something bigger."

Oh, really.

"I'm the same," says the manicurist, "I want to open my own clinic. You can't work too long for someone else if you have what it takes to be an entrepreneur."

Carolyn hmmms, and I smile, imagining how she feels having her ambition to be Condé Nast's creative director compared to the manicurist's desire to own a nails and wax emporium.

We hear the rattling sound of a nail polish bottle being shaken. "Look," the manicurist says, "you and I want to get somewhere, but some people, well . . ." She lowers her voice, though not low enough. "I see that here. Women in a rut who aren't brave enough to go out on their own. You know?"

Elsa's eyes meet mine for a millisecond, then slide away.

Carolyn's voice. "I know someone exactly like that where I work. I used to think she was a threat, but she's going nowhere fast. She's stuck in the same old groove."

She can't mean me. She does, the bitch. I can't believe it.

Elsa says, "All done," and leaves the room. I quickly get dressed, wondering how I can sneak out without seeing Carolyn.

"There. Good as new," says the talky woman next door. "Now we can do your pedicure."

Thank you, Carolyn. I slip through the door and scoot out of the salon, though not without leaving Elsa a generous tip in exchange for her silence.

By the time I boarded the plane for London a few days later, not only was I waxed, but my body was toned and dieted (within its pear-shaped limits), my hair was freshly trimmed and deep-conditioned, and I was clothed with my version of elegance and understatement in case I might run into Brian somewhere. Anywhere.

Not to worry, though, because he wasn't around. Not in London, anyway. And neither was Carolyn, hardly. Oh, she made the trip all right, but Marni and I barely saw her. Guess her ambitions included a possible international connection — you've never seen anyone network like she networked. Milan was pretty much the same story: Carolyn flitting about and Brian not present. Which really tipped the odds against his coming to Paris.

By the time we arrived in France, I was exhausted anyway, and fed up, and had developed a serious yearning for private time. I escaped to my room when we checked into our Paris hotel — I couldn't wait to lie down with a cool cloth over my forehead. But as I stood in the hallway outside my door, my shaking-with-fatigue hands searching for the room key I'd been given only five minutes before, it occurred to me that maybe Brian was in town. And if he were, maybe he would have sent me flowers. A hope against all reason, but there it is.

I rummaged through my purse for the key and visualized an expensive arrangement of wild roses in rich shades of yellow, pink, and peach. Or maybe an extravagant bunch of white freesia, the ends of each bloom tipped in lavender, the lot tied up with a purple ribbon.

Carolyn's voice chirped through my reverie. "Hi, Rosemary. Looks like we'll be side by side."

"Great," I said. And the key fell out of my mouth and onto the floor. I picked it up and unlocked the door.

GET WITH IT, KIDDO. Reality was Carolyn on the other side of the wall, listening to my toilet flush. Kill the fantasy: there would be no Brian, no romance, and no flowers this trip.

Only there were some. Three different arrangements. A pot of violets, a multicoloured assortment involving chrysanthemums, and a sheaf of wheat. I strolled over, very casual, and read the cards. The wheat was from a lesser-known French designer we'd featured last season, the mums were from a Canadian trade commissioner, and the violets were from the hotel. How thoughtful.

I undressed, lay down on the bed, and closed my eyes. Models immediately began race-walking through my head to sped-up house music. I tipped that image into the garbage can and tried to construct something more peaceful. To classical music, maybe. I filled my mind with a Strauss waltz. My breathing slowed and my body sagged into the mattress. The music swelled, and I cued the dancers to sail onto centre stage. I fell asleep spinning in the grand ballroom at Versailles, my taffeta and tulle skirt twirling, in my eyes a look of adoration aimed at my faceless partner.

I spotted Brian as soon as Carolyn, Marni, and I walked into an industry party held that night at a cavernous nightclub. He was leaning against the opposite wall, deep in conversation with a woman I recognized — a senior executive from Neiman-Marcus. And he looked as handsome as ever, in a dark grey suit and a blue-grey silk shirt buttoned to the neck.

I took a quick swipe under the eyes with a fingertip, trawling for smudged eyeliner. Good thing my dress was not only unwrinkled but also figure-flattering, appropriate and black.

I grabbed a glass of wine from a passing waiter's tray, said to Carolyn and Marni, "I think I'll mingle," and took off. I toured the room, saying hello and chatting briefly with people I knew, and followed a roundabout route that would eventually position me close to Brian and far from Carolyn and Marni. I made my way at last to the ideal location and was lucky to find nearby a fashion writer acquaintance from Chicago, with whom I was able to engage in bright conversation while I watched Brian out of the corner of my eye and waited for an opportunity to throw myself in his path.

But my peripheral vision wasn't what it used to be, because the next time I did a discreet head turn in Brian's direction, he was gone. With great self-control, I waited for Chicago to finish up her anecdote so I could break away for an all-out manhunt.

And boy did I jump when Brian's arm slid around my waist a minute later.

"Hello there." I'd aimed for a cool, aloof tone, but my voice came out squeaky.

He nodded at Chicago. "Would you excuse us? Business."

He pulled me out of the room by the hand and opened the first door in the hallway, which led to a fancy private telephone room. He shut the door behind us, sat me down in the chair and perched on the corner of the desktop.

"Hello," he said. "You look lovely, Rosie."

Rosie? No one called me Rosie. I cleared my throat of an enormous chunk of nervousness. "So do you. Look lovely, I mean." His skin was so pink, his hair so chestnutty.

He leaned closer. "Would you think it terribly forward of me . . ."

I couldn't help it — I licked my lips.

"Would you mind awfully if I . . ." He pulled me to my feet facing him, reached behind my head, and gathered up my hair in his hands. I closed my eyes and moved my face toward his.

"I've waited so long for this," he whispered just before he kissed me, just before I dived into a deep dark pool where there are no long-suffering wives and no good-looking philandering cads and no love-starved single women infatuated with a dream of their own making.

So he was a perfect kisser. First of all, he tasted good. Not like mouthwash or mints, more like a single malt scotch with some smoke around the edges. And the technique was there, too. None of that mouth-open-too-wide-tongue-halfway-down-your-throat-and-pumping routine. Instead, soft lips firmly attached to mine, the right amount of wetness without slobber, a subtle hint of tongue. Good arm and hand work, too — one hand creeping up my side, the other cradling my head.

Meanwhile, I wasn't exactly standing around like a limp piece of overcooked linguine. Aside from my momentary blackout when we first kissed and the dancing white lights I saw behind my eyelids, I was right in there — yanking his shirttails out of his pants, running my hands up his back, pressing body.

In fact, my hand was circling his belt buckle, beginning the descent for landing, when he kissed me behind the ear and whispered, "Let's get out of here."

I struggled to open my eyes and stood there, swaying on my high heels, while he pulled out a handkerchief and gently dabbed away at the smeared lipstick on my mouth and his. The damage repaired, he led me into the brightly lit lobby, placed his hand on the small of my back, and guided me out the door and into a cab. "*Le George V, s'il vous plait*," he said, and draped an arm along the back of the seat.

The driver grunted, flicked the meter on, and pulled away from the corner, fast. My head was thrown back, grazing Brian's sleeve, and while part of me wanted to lean back into the crook of that arm as a way of rubbing together any available body parts, another part of me still felt like I'd been riding the Tilt-A-Whirl — dizzy passion on top of travel fatigue was making me a little nauseous.

Mind you, sitting close to Brian, our thighs touching, kept me fairly alert, and opening the window to let some cool fall air wash over my overheated face helped, but I did hope the cab ride would be short — I could feel carsickness hovering nearby. Are we there yet? I wanted to ask, because I had a feeling that even if I didn't vomit, there was still the embarrassing possibility of leaving a wet spot on the car seat.

The drive from A to B probably only took about ten minutes, but it felt longer. I was too dizzy to talk, the driver stayed mute, and

Brian maintained a stony façade until, about halfway into the drive, I began to wonder if I'd imagined the fervent necking back at the club, and if I was wrong in assuming that anything further in the sex line was going to transpire that evening.

Because, aside from the thigh contact, there was no indication of fun to come from Brian — he wasn't whispering sweet nothings in my ear, nor did he have his hand up my skirt doing interesting things to my nether regions, though he could have without the driver noticing. Except he couldn't have, because I was wearing pantyhose, not having anticipated an opportunity for his hand to be up my skirt, though I *will* admit to having slipped a condom into my evening bag.

Not that I even own a garter belt or stockings. It was just that Brian was not showing a great deal of visible lust, when he had the chance. I tried peeking at his crotch to see if the rocklike appendage he'd pressed against me in the telephone room was still standing, but the cab was dark, his legs were crossed, the cloth of his pants was draped in his lap — I couldn't tell.

The hotel loomed up ahead. Brian said to the driver, "*Par là, au coin, ça va, merci,*" dug into his pocket for some money, paid, and escorted me out of the cab.

We seemed to be at a side entrance of the hotel. He guided me again, with the hand-on-the-back business, through the doors, across the lobby, and into an elevator manned by a operator who nodded at him and pressed the button for the top floor without being told the number.

Before the door closed, some prosperous-looking American men in suits came on board, talking about dinner plans. Dinner? Shit, it wasn't even eight o'clock yet and here I'd been thinking we were going to bed already. Unless I was wrong.

Brian said, in a low voice, "I picked up the last issue of *Panache*. There were some provocative ideas there."

I looked into his eyes, searching for some irony, but saw no twinkle. "Yeah? Name one."

He spoke a touch louder. "There was a story on suits I quite liked. Shot in the business district, in black-and-white, with skyscrapers in the background. Moody. And the beauty pages design was fresh. What's the name of the art director again?"

"Carolyn Whiting. Why?"

"I like to collect the names of people who do good work. You never know when our paths might cross."

"In that case, I'll have to introduce you to her tomorrow. She's here in Paris." I made a face.

"I take it you don't like her style?"

We'd reached the penthouse level. I stepped out and turned back to Brian. "Her work's okay. It's her personal style I can't stand. We're, like, total opposites."

Brian frowned, guided me to the right, and reached for his key. I heard the elevator doors close behind us. "I never allow temperamental differences to colour my opinion of someone's talent," he said. He unlocked the door of the suite, flicked on the lights, and ushered me into a large sitting room — all cream silk brocade and dark wood.

"Well," I said, "*I* never tell people how to think when I don't know the whole story. So I guess you and I are different."

He walked over to a bar, stepped behind it, and opened cupboard doors. When he spoke, his voice was mild. "Would you care for a drink?"

No, I didn't want a drink. I wanted to wind the tape back about a half hour. I wanted to be washed away in the throes of passion, not be talking about Carolyn. Besides, the crotch of my underwear was turning hard and crusty and starting to chafe. I sat down on a gilt and brocade chair and winced. "Would you mind telling me what we're doing here?"

He came around the bar, handed me a glass of cognac, and sat down on a matching chair. Muted music had started playing in the background — the Gypsy Kings, it sounded like.

He clinked his glass against mine. "Here's to a splendid night of lovemaking, I hope." He drank.

My anger vanished and my underpants softened. I sipped the cognac.

Brian leaned over — so cool, so confident — and kissed my collarbone. Between kisses he said, "My apologies for the shop talk in the elevator."

I put down my glass, reached for his shirt collar, undid the top button and slipped my hand inside. God, he had a great neck. By the time his mouth reached my lips, I'd unbuttoned three more of his buttons and forgiven all, if only because I was incapable of anything resembling rational thought.

Okay. Here's the full dirt: well, pretty full, anyway. The first run-through got animalistic fast, featuring lots of grunts and moans (from me, at least) and tearing at each other's clothes. Forget foreplay — it was straight to the main event, in three different positions.

After that first frantic time, we came up for air and I mentioned I was hungry. So he ordered up some lobster mayonnaise and champagne. When the food arrived, I ate, he drank, and, that done with, we got down to the serious lovemaking: the slow stuff, the "Do you like it this way, or that way?" stuff. Which was beyond wonderful — picture me faint with rapture — except for the noise thing.

I know it's rather vulgar, but I do like to make noise when I'm enjoying myself. And when we got around to my first orgasm of the evening, I was ready to lift off the roof with my scream. I started building up to it with moans and cries, but, just before I got there, I felt Brian's hand placed gently on my mouth and heard his voice in my ear whispering, "Quietly, now." I proceeded to pantomime my cries, which meant I still felt like the solar system had shifted, though maybe not as much as if I'd been able to herald the event in full voice.

And there was a marked silence on his part, too. I mean, I could tell he was having fun, but when he came, there would be an extreme shuddering and a deep exhalation, and I'd think — I guess that was it, then. And it struck me as slightly weird, his total silence. That is, it struck me as a bit weird later, when I had time to think about it, when I wasn't in the middle of panting and snorting.

Around midnight, I surveyed my body condition and decided a rinse in the bidet wasn't up to the job — I'd better retreat to my own hotel room, hose myself down and sleep there. A concept which met with no opposition when I suggested it to Brian, though I may have imagined hearing him heave a sign of relief.

He got dressed and came down in the elevator with me, and held open the door of the cab he'd arranged to have waiting. "Good-night," he said. "I'll look for you tomorrow. I don't know how I'll be able to keep my hands off you in public."

It was only later, after I'd showered, brushed my teeth, applied an ice pack to my swollen mouth, and briefly considered applying it to my other lips, that I heard his words again in my mind. It was only after I'd pulled on my pyjamas, snuggled into bed and started to fall asleep, without building a dream for once, that I realized what those words meant: Quietly, now. Don't forget he knows people. Don't forget he's married.

Chapter Six

I walked into the Foulnier show at the Plaza Athénée the next morning almost late, what with having spent extra time on hair and makeup and changing my clothes twice before I'd settled on which combination of my many black separates struck just the right morning-after note. I spotted Brian right away, standing at his seat, one foot on the chair rung, facing the back rows. He caught my eye and made a gesture with his head that was so subtle I wasn't sure he'd made it at all.

I sat down beside Marni and Carolyn and made my voice sound weak. "Hi, guys."

"How are you feeling?" Marni asked.

I'd already squirmed out of breakfast by leaving her a note saying I wasn't well, they should go on without me. I tried looking sick. "Better than last night, but not great."

Carolyn's head turned my way. "What happened last night?"

"I was sick. Grossly sick. Bilious liquids coming out both ends — totally disgusting."

"Really?" Marni said.

"It might have been the crab mousse canapés. Did you two have any? No? Lucky. I barely made it back to the hotel before I started puking. And the vomit was this Day-Glo shade of yellow, with green flecks in it — parsley, I guess — the whole thing looked a bit like a curry, come to think of it, and — "

Marni held up her hand. "We get the picture. Sounds awful. Strange, though, that when I got in at eleven, the concierge said you were out."

"I sort of crawled along the floor past his desk. I guess he didn't see me."

"I knocked on your door."

"I was pretty well passed out. Though I did have the weirdest dream, about carpentry, of all things. Nails being pounded into wood, over and over. Maybe that was you, knocking."

"You've got to hand it to Ivana — look at that hair," said Carolyn.

I searched out Ivana Trump's blonde beehive in the crowd. "Hey, Marni, how about we feature that as hairstyle of the month?"

"No."

Phew. Subject changed. And a minute later the lights went down. I peered into the dark until I could make out the back of Brian's head, several rows up and a bunch of people to the right. I gazed at the nape of his neck and felt again his skin under my fingers. I pulled my jacket closer around me and sat back to watch the show.

Afterwards, Marni stayed put, making her famous notes, but I jumped up and joined the exiting throng, eager to go make goo-goo eyes with Brian. The procession moved slowly out the ballroom doors and down the corridor. There he was . . . up ahead in the crowd . . . oh, lost him . . . no, there he was again. I weaved in and out through the crowd. The line of people broke through to the lobby and I finally came within touching distance. Not that I planned to, but I could have reached out and plucked at his sleeve. Except I didn't, because Carolyn was plucking at *my* sleeve. "So, Rosemary," she said, "What stood out for you from that show?"

I watched Brian walk across the lobby and vanish into the newsstand, feeling like Lieutenant Gerard seeing The Fugitive slip through his fingers. "Sorry?"

"The show we just saw — what was significant there, in your opinion?"

This was a good question, because at that moment I could not recall a single garment. Being up late the night before, that achy feeling between the legs, the dark room — had I actually dozed off? "Oh, you know, not much."

Irritation flickered across her forehead. I'd have to try harder. I kept an eye on the door of the newsstand and searched in the brain for any shred of a stored image. Wait. I remembered one. "The silver satin bride's dress was fairly fab."

Carolyn's brow evened out and she smiled. "Yeah. I could see myself in that dress."

This seemed to be going a little far in terms of presumption, as Claudia Schiffer had been the bride and the dress a body-hugging mini. "Funny," I said, "you don't strike me as the marrying kind."

"How are you feeling, by the way, Rosemary? You appear to have made a miraculous recovery."

I feigned agony and noticed that Brian had come back out into the lobby and was leaning against a column, beating time on the open palm of one hand with a rolled-up magazine he held in the other.

"Actually," I said to Carolyn, "I'm still a little shaky." I placed a hand over my stomach. "I'd better go to the washroom." And pass Brian on the way.

I wrinkled my nose to suggest this was a trip better taken alone, but she said, "I'll come with you. Where is it?"

Damn. I headed off, tailed by Carolyn. And when we'd passed Brian, he called out, "Excuse me, Rosemary?"

I whipped around.

"Hello," he said to Carolyn. "I'm Brian Turnbull, how do you do?"

"Well, how do *you* do?" she said.

No. She couldn't, she wouldn't —

"I'm Carolyn Whiting," she said, "*Panache* magazine. And I can't believe Rosemary has been keeping a handsome man like you a secret." She admonished me with her index finger but looked only at him.

Brian smiled faintly and caught my eye. "Wasn't it you last night at the cocktail party who said you'd never seen *Fashion Folio*?"

I stared at him. Huh?

He handed me the rolled-up magazine. "I brought along a copy for you. Feel free to subscribe."

I took the magazine from him and mumbled thanks. I wanted to give him a what-the-hell-and-when-will-I-see-you-next look, but I couldn't get his attention, so busy was he telling Carolyn nice to have met her and running off without a backward glance.

I headed for the washroom, Carolyn in tow. "Now *how* do you know him?"

I opened the washroom door and motioned her inside. "You come to enough of these things, you meet just about everybody." We joined a short line-up for a toilet stall.

Carolyn lowered her voice. "He's the one with the empire, right? How many magazines does he own?"

"I don't know. Five? Six?" The line moved. She was next.

She turned back to me and reached for the magazine. "Can I see that one?"

I tightened my grip as the next stall became available. "Do you mind if I just . . . ?" I pushed past her. "You know, my stomach." I nipped inside and locked the door. I threw my bag on the floor, lowered the lid of the toilet seat, sat down and unrolled the magazine. Okay, what was going on here?

I checked the cover — nothing remarkable. I turned to the table of contents and scanned the article headings but found no clue there. I flipped through the beauty ads in the front, waiting for inspiration to strike. Nope. I turned to the centrefold and saw a cream-coloured envelope taped to the page.

Above the noise of flushing toilets, I heard Carolyn in the next stall saying something about coffee, the first worthwhile words she'd spoken that morning, it seemed to me. I flushed my own toilet and ripped open the envelope.

Inside was a single sheet of creamy paper, letterhead from a Left Bank hotel I'd never heard of. Taped to the paper was a key, and written in that art director's handwriting were the words "Room 20. 16:00."

I tucked the envelope and contents into my bag and came out of the stall. Carolyn was already at the sink.

"Did I hear you mention coffee?" I said. "Because I could really go for a café au lait right now."

"Sure. And I'd like to take a look at that copy of *Fashion Folio*. Why'd he give it to you again?"

For the rest of the day, it was almost like every other trip to the collections. I regained my ability to absorb the sight of clothes, and I hung out with my usual crowd, Carolyn and Marni included. And throughout the day I saw Brian. Saw him sitting in the front row conferring with an earnest young assistant. Saw him chatting during the breaks with his editors, saw him hanging with some industry bigwigs.

But we didn't speak. I could see, from the studious way he avoided eye contact whenever I "happened" to look his way, that there would be no more subtle nods, no more notes passed. It was like we'd never even met. Though we had, and publicly — the dinner in New York, the cocktail reception only the night before. How come it was okay to chat then and now we had to act like strangers?

Still, I had four o'clock to look forward to, and not much time to worry about Brian. I was busy enough imprinting show images on the brain, analyzing audience reaction, and occasionally remembering to act sick. After the two o'clock, I pleaded illness and returned to the hotel, where I ripped off my clothes, took my third shower in twenty-four hours, changed into a T-shirt, jeans, cowboy boots and black leather jacket, and went back out.

The cab pulled up in front of a solid old five-storey building that overlooked a small square. Inside, the clerk behind the front desk nodded at me and said, "*Bonjour, mademoiselle.*" I blurted out the line

I'd prepared about a business meeting and was directed up two flights of stairs and to my left. I climbed the steep circular staircase, feeling more than a bit silly — I kept wondering when I'd be handed the briefcase containing either the secret documents or a fortune in heroin — and hesitated before the door to Room 20. I unlocked the door and walked in.

The room was certainly bigger than mine, but nothing like Brian's fancy suite at the George V. A quick look around revealed pink and white floral wallpaper, sunlight beaming in through small white frame windows, real flowers glowing in window boxes. Oh, yeah, and a big canopied bed made up with white cotton bed linens.

Brian was standing at the window, leaning on a desk, looking out, and talking on a cellular phone. He still wore that morning's clothes — pleated trousers in a French blue, a pale blue cotton shirt, an arty tie in yellows and oranges. His jacket was arranged across the back of a chair.

He smiled at me and waved and kept talking — I heard the words "sell," "exchange," and "fund" repeated a few times. He gestured to me to sit. I started to slip off my jacket, decided to keep it on, and sat down.

"Fine, then. Goodbye." He set down the phone. "Hello, Rosie."

"You didn't ask me the password."

He unbuttoned his cuffs and rolled up his sleeves. "Do you know I've thought of nothing but you since last night?"

And you gotta admire a guy with the balls to utter a line like that, don't you? Especially when it was obvious he'd been thinking for at least the last few minutes about his investments. I stood up and walked over to a spot beside him at the window. "See anything you liked today?"

"Only you."

So corny! But I fell for it. He moved behind me, slipped my jacket off my shoulders, threw it on the bed, and circled my waist with his arms. I leaned back and rested my head against his shoulder for a minute, wishing all the tiny hairs on my skin would lie down already. And that went for the goosebumps as well.

I turned to face him with my eyes closed, began kissing him, unbuckled my belt, unzipped my jeans and let them fall. Only they got stuck on my hips, so I broke the lip contact and wriggled and pushed until the jeans slid to my knees. Except I forgot I had cowboy boots on, so there I stood with my jeans scrunched up around the top of my boots. All I wanted to do was worship at the Brian sex altar, but instead I had to bend down and take off the boots, something impossible to do while standing.

"Fuck," I said. I sat down on the floor and tugged.

"Need some help with that?" He was laughing, the bum.

I glared and shook my head, so he sat on the bed and took off his shoes and unbuttoned his shirt while I pulled and panted and finally jumped up, clad in T-shirt, underpants and white sweat socks. "Ta-da!"

He leaned over, nuzzled me, and said, "I like the socks. Will you keep them on?"

I lay in bed, dozing. Brian stepped out of the bathroom, a towel around his waist. "I have to leave," he said, "but stay as long as you like."

I yawned and sat up. "So what's the deal here?"

"Deal?"

"How many hotel rooms do you have around Paris? Where're we going to meet tomorrow?" Pretty nervy there, mentioning the future, I know, but I'd heard him utter a strangled kind of gasp once during our lovemaking, so I'd become cocky.

He came over and sat beside me on the bed. "You're not keen on the sneaking around."

"Did I say that? I didn't say that. It's kind of fun. I feel like Leslie Howard in *The Scarlet Pimpernel*."

"I'm afraid I have to be discreet."

I rolled over. "I know. But it was weird today seeing you and feeling like I'm supposed to pretend we've never met. And not knowing what was going to happen here today at 16:00 hours. Maybe it was all a white slavery set-up, you know? Or yellow slavery, whatever."

He leaned down and kissed me. "You're marvellous."

I blushed. "Gee, thanks, but what *is* the deal?"

He stood up and started to dress. "I've booked this room for the week, for us. We can meet here, once a day if it can be managed, maybe even twice. Not just for sex. We could have some food brought in. We could talk. How does that sound?"

"As long as I can shake Carolyn and Marni, it sounds good."

"Carolyn, the art director?"

"That's the one. I think she liked you. She mentioned over coffee you were kind of cute for a guy your age."

He winced. "Yes, well, I'm meeting her for a drink later."

My heart stopped beating. "You're what?"

"She rang me at my hotel, left a message asking to meet. Said she wanted to pick my brain." He smiled, the rogue again. "Claimed I was legendary in art director circles."

I made a fist and pounded my chest to restart my pulse. Could any male on earth resist Carolyn's wiles?

Marni and I were sitting in our seats for the eight o'clock show, in fatigued silence, when Carolyn sashayed in, doll-like in a YSL knockoff, full makeup, and freshly sprayed hair. I bit my tongue and nudged Marni. Marni looked Carolyn up and down. "Going out tonight?"

Carolyn sat. "Just meeting someone for a drink."

I watched her face. "Anyone we know?"

"I'll be right back," she said and went off to chat with a British fashion editor she'd met in London. She timed her return to coincide with the show's start and left before the applause had died down.

"I think I'm going to skip the ten o'clock," Marni said.

"Me too." I needed to sleep, badly.

"And I'm sure Carolyn won't be making it."

"Why do you say that?"

"You know who she's meeting? Brian Turnbull."

"Oh, come on. They'll probably have some boring discussion about graphic design."

Marni laughed. "We *are* talking about Carolyn, aren't we?"

I faked a laugh, too.

And damn if I didn't lay awake in my hotel room waiting to hear the sound of her footstep outside my door, the click of a key in her lock. When it finally came, I looked at my clock for the six-hundredth time. One a.m. Time enough for anything.

I'd been hoping I could count on Marni to question Carolyn the next morning when we sat, in various stages of blear, in the hotel's breakfast room, drinking coffee and nibbling at croissants.

Marni was certainly the best-rested. "How was your date with Brian Turnbull, Carolyn?"

Carolyn glanced at me before answering. What did *that* mean? "It wasn't a date." Another look at me. "He's quite married, unfortunately."

I signalled to the waiter for more coffee and uttered some of the lines I'd worked up the night before when I'd been lying awake in bed. "He's quite the charmer though, isn't he? Too bad he's got the WASPy kind of looks that fade with age."

Carolyn regarded me with interest. "How well do you know him, Rosemary?"

Careful now. Maybe she's asked him the same question. And what would he have answered?

Marni, to my rescue. "We run into him here and there." She turned to me. "Didn't he invite you and Helen to dinner in New York last season?"

"That one, or the one before. Who can remember?"

Carolyn stirred sweetener into her coffee. "Why would he want to meet you and Helen?"

I swallowed some indignation and summoned up a shrug. "I guess he wants to meet everyone at least once. You know, networking. So, what are we seeing first today, again?"

Marni said, "LaCroix. Then Gaultier." She pulled the schedule out of her bag.

"Well," Carolyn said, "I told Brian if he ever comes to Toronto to give me a call, stop by for a visit."

Marni looked up. "Why?"

"So I can show him around *Panache*, of course."

It was Marni's turn to shrug. "Don't know why he'd be interested in that."

As the week in Paris flew by, dodging Marni and Carolyn became less of a problem — after ten days together on the road, I wasn't the only one needing a break. So, in between shows, Brian and I managed to meet and make love every day. We even had time to chat a bit about work — mine, mostly. He asked me about *Panache*, about its reporting structure, how editorial decisions were made, what I thought our distinctive characteristics were, what our potential was — things I'd never really discussed with anyone outside work, and never so openly. And it was fun to speak my mind on the subject, knowing it didn't matter what I said. Who could be farther removed from the reality of day-to-day *Panache* operations than Brian, and yet still understand and, apparently, be interested?

Fast as the time passed, I didn't worry about it ending soon, because I figured we'd meet in New York in a few weeks for the

American collections (time enough to get waxed again — how convenient) and carry on, in a different city, a different hotel room.

But on our last night in Paris, as we lay in bed, he said, "I can't make it to New York this season. I have business in Sydney that can't wait."

I turned on my side, away from him.

He turned, too, and started plaiting my hair into skinny little braids which were hell to untie later.

"I'll have to find business that takes me to Toronto," he said. "Don't you think?"

I didn't answer. I remembered after the sailing night, when he'd said he'd keep in touch and hadn't. And I remembered how Carolyn was planning to show him around *Panache* next time he came to town. I felt a tension ache flaring up in my neck and shoulders. Might as well deal with it right now.

"You know last spring," I said, "in New York, when you introduced yourself to me?"

"I remember it well. You wore black."

"Why did you approach me, though, that day? What made you invite me along?"

"Because," he said, "in that room full of beautiful, vacuous women, your intelligence shone out like a beacon and drew me to you, a boat to harbour."

I sighed. "You're so full of shit."

He started stroking the top of my shoulder, down my arm, and back up. The kind of featherlight strokes like that game where you close your eyes and try to guess when someone's touched the soft spot on the inside of your elbow. "But Brian, really, why did you?" I turned around to face him.

He closed his eyes for a long moment, then opened them and looked straight at me. When he spoke, his voice was quiet and clear. "I saw you in New York, and I remembered noticing you the season before, in Paris. You'd caught my eye from across the room — a striking young woman with masses of beautiful hair. I found out who you were. I had to meet you." He rolled over on top of me and took his weight on his elbows. "So that one day I could make love to you like this."

He slowly eased inside me. Then out, just as slow. Then in. I shuddered and stared at his brilliant eyes, wide open above me. I began to moan.

"Quietly, now," he whispered.

Chapter Seven

The Toronto winter dragged by, spring returned, and the *Panache* group migrated to New York for the fall collections. On our first day, we elected to do the downtown scene as part of our show-the-new-publisher-the-fashion-sights tour. For Campbell Cameron was gone at last, replaced by one Elizabeth Crowley, fortyish, American. Still naive after all these years, I'd barged into Marni's office as soon as word got out, the press release about Elizabeth in hand. "So this is good news, right? If she worked on *Contemporary Woman* and *Show Biz Weekly*, she must really know what she's doing."

Marni barely looked at me, just kept on with her paperwork. "Grow up, Rosemary."

"I've caught you at a bad time."

"Can't you see they're all the same, these business people, no matter where they're from?"

"I thought — "

"You thought things might change? Nothing changes unless *you* change it. When are you going to figure that out?"

For a second there I expected her eyes to go vampirish, or smoke to start pouring from the palms of her hands. But at least she hadn't directed her wrath at me. "I take it you're not hosting the welcome party?"

She hadn't answered, had merely dismissed me, and had acted more than usually touchy ever since.

And now I found myself face-to-hair with our fair leader in the crammed freight elevator taking the *Panache* crew and a bunch of other fashion followers up to the loft of a hot new downtown designer.

The elevator disgorged us on the sixth floor, where, as per plan, Simon Wong, our photographer, headed straight into the show space, brandishing his pass. Marni and Elizabeth took up a waiting position leaning against a wall, and Helen and I ran for the press table to join the crowd shouting and waving invitations in the faces of the two girls behind the desk.

In the midst of the mosh pit, some jerk behind me stepped on my heel. I turned to give him a dirty look, and that's when I saw Brian, farther back, getting off the elevator with a clutch of new arrivals.

My insides instantly went into the spin cycle. Amazing how he still had that effect on me, even though we'd trysted four times in the last six months, in every fashion capital going. Without exactly waving, I tried to catch his eye, but I was pretty well buried in the crush — he couldn't see me. That was okay, though, because our next assignation was all set — prearranged by phone the week before. We were to meet this very night at six, at an Upper East Side apartment hotel.

I turned my attention back to my place in line and saw that I was almost within reach of the table girl. Too bad she was preoccupied, listening to a security guard who knelt beside her and talked into her ear.

"Oh, come on," someone in front of me said, and "For Christ's sake," yelled another.

She ignored them, bent her head, checked her lists, found a name, wrote something on a piece of paper and handed it to the guard.

The jockeying for position restarted, but I held still and watched the security guard go, curious to see who was getting the VIP treatment. The guard walked over to the wall where Brian stood, the ubiquitous female assistant at his side. The guard handed Brian the paper, Brian thanked him, slipped him a bill, and turned back to his conversation with — would you believe — Elizabeth and Marni.

From where I stood, Elizabeth looked animated, Marni guarded, Brian gorgeous. What could *that* be about?

Helen was beside me. "I got our numbers!" she said. We struggled through the crowd and stumbled out into the small space near Elizabeth and Marni.

"Later, then," Brian said to Elizabeth. His eyes passed over Helen and me, he nodded at us, and he left.

"What did he want?" Helen asked Elizabeth.

"Brian Turnbull? You know him? He stopped by to say hello — we're old friends. Actually, he's invited us all out tonight. He has a block of tickets to *Guys and Dolls*. Would you girls like to go?"

Helen looked at me. "It would only mean missing Amelia Richardson's show. What do you think?"

My mind was whirling. Sex at six, show at eight? Kind of tight, wasn't it? And why had he invited the *Panache* group anyway?

I turned to Marni. "Amelia's stuff was pretty old last time. And we could send Simon to get some film, just in case."

Marni stared at me hard, and when she spoke, her tone was sarcastic. "Whatever you say, Rosemary."

Now what?

The last show of our afternoon ended at 4:45. Barely enough time to run up to the hotel, change, and take a cab to meet Brian. We filed out of the New York Hilton. "I'm walking back," I announced.

Elizabeth said, "I'll see you all at the theatre at 7:45," and strode off. One down.

"I'll walk up with you, Rosemary," Helen said. "And I might squeeze in a workout at the hotel exercise room. Want to?"

I shook my head and set off at a fast pace. "No thanks. I think I'll just flake out, maybe take a nap."

Marni's voice called out from behind us. "Wait up, Rosemary."

Helen and I stopped and waited, then marched off again with Marni half-running alongside.

"You two are in an awful hurry," Marni said. "Rosemary, I thought we might sit down together back at the hotel and talk over what we've seen today."

Since when did we ever do this? "Actually," I said, "I'm meeting a friend for a drink, so I'll have to pass."

Helen gave me a look.

Marni said, "What friend?"

Shit. "A friend from high school. I haven't seen her in years, since she moved down here." We walked by a bookstore window featuring a display of self-help books. "She's in publishing. Non-fiction."

Helen gave me another look.

"Will we meet you at the theatre, then?" Marni said.

Relief. Two down. "Good idea."

We arrived at the hotel. "Hey, Rosemary," said Helen, "I was wondering if I could borrow that book you were reading on the plane. For the exercise bike. Do you mind?"

"Sure. Come on up. See you later, Marni."

The book was on my bedside table — it was a Maeve Binchy, a warm-hearted novel, set in an Irish village, which my mother had given me for Christmas. Not Helen's type of thing, I would have thought. I handed it over. Helen took it and sat down on my bed. My eyes strayed to the clock on the TV. "I should call my friend." I pulled my address book out of my bag and started searching for an imaginary phone number.

"Where are you really going?" Helen said.

I shut the address book and sat down next to her. "Helen, I . . . look, I . . . okay, I'll tell you the truth. But you can't breathe a word. To anyone. Promise?"

"Cross my heart."

"I'm meeting Brian Turnbull."

Helen picked at the bedcover. "Why are you meeting him?"

I stood up, pulled out my makeup bag, and walked over to the mirror. "God, this is so embarrassing. I'm meeting him because we're having an affair."

Helen smiled. "No! Hey, lucky you."

I dusted my face with powder. "It's just a fling. Except you really can't let on, because he's totally into secrecy."

She came up behind me, looked in the mirror, and finger-combed her own hair. "Well, I wouldn't have guessed. I thought maybe you were job-hunting."

"That's the last thing on my mind."

"Why? Don't you think we've been at *Panache* long enough?"

"Job-hunting. That's a good one."

"But if you did start looking around, you'd tell me, right?"

I put down my makeup. "Okay, sure."

"Good." She walked over to the door. "See you later." She winked. "Have fun." The door shut behind her.

Three down, none to go.

The apartment hotel Brian had chosen for our rendezvous was sedate but tasteful, with its grey carpet, grey-and-white striped bed linens, pale grey slipcovered chairs. Very quiet, too. As quiet as, well, as quiet as Brian. Up in that room on the thirtieth floor, you'd never know there was crazed rush-hour traffic several stories down or that anyone else was even in the building.

Not that I put the padded-cell silence to the test when I had a chance. No, I'd learned how to keep quiet and did so, despite Round One of sex being of the cock-a-doodle-do variety.

After, I lay in bed beside him, cooling down. Between healing breaths, I said, "Okay, two questions."

"Hello to you, too."

I touched the cleft in his chin. "Hi. First question: What's the story on inviting the *Panache* crowd out tonight?"

He sat up and reached for the remote. He flicked on the TV,

muted the volume, and found a stock market channel. "You know how I like to keep in touch, meet people."

"Not that networking crap again. Come on."

He flicked the TV off and started fooling with my hair. "Really," I said, "why are we going to *Guys and Dolls*?"

"So I can see more of you. I'll arrange it so we sit together, as if by chance, of course."

"What you really mean is you'll act like we've never met."

He leaned down and kissed me, a long, dreamy one that made my questions float away. When we became unglued, he moved his head down and started kissing my shoulders. "Did you have another question?"

I closed my eyes and shook my head. Later. I'd find out how he knew Elizabeth Crowley later.

We left the hotel separately, at timed intervals, and took separate cabs down, Brian and I, but I jumped out of mine on Broadway at 49th Street. Too much traffic. Besides, the walk would put some colour in my cheeks and a sparkle in my eye, or at least give me a good excuse for having both already.

Too bad I met Marni charging into Times Square. "Hi," she said. "How'd it go with your high school friend?"

"Oh, fine. We got caught up, talked about old times."

"Where'd you go?"

Where'd we go. "Some bar downtown near her office with an Irish name — O'Malley's? Shea's? Something like that."

"And which publisher does she work for?"

"I've never heard of it. It's a small press called Crazy Lady Publishing. Have *you* heard of it?"

"No." She stayed quiet for a few steps while I congratulated myself on my improvising. Crazy lady indeed.

"How gallant of Brian Turnbull to invite us all out this evening," she said next. "He really seems to bond with *Panache* people — you and Helen, Carolyn."

"Supposed to be a great show though — do you know if Nathan Lane and Faith Prince are still in it?"

"Why'd he ask us, do you think, when he could invite anyone?"

"Maybe everyone else was busy?"

She didn't smile. "Have you had many conversations with him?"

"Me?"

"I just wondered if he'd ever asked you about business, about things like, oh, like *Panache's* financial performance, for instance."

Brian and I *had* touched on that topic, oddly enough, the last time we'd met, which was — let's see — back in January. Just before Campbell Cameron left, when Brian had surprised me one day in Toronto, calling up at the last minute and asking me to come up to the Four Seasons Hotel.

It was then, when we'd been getting undressed, that he'd mentioned one of his publications was having financial problems, and I'd thrown in about how we'd had to cut editorial pages at *Panache* on the next quarter's issues because the ad revenues were down, which was a total drag, and he'd asked how bad was it, exactly, did I know?

I guess I *had* thought it a little strange to be discussing numbers with Brian. But surely that had just been chitchat, him trying to take an interest in my humdrum life. Hadn't it? God, Marni was making me paranoid, like her.

"I've barely talked to Brian Turnbull about anything," I said.

"Well, don't forget: loose lips sink ships. One must be careful."

One? Who's one, white man?

Guys and Dolls was great.

The only sour note was Marni making an announcement at intermission when Brian went off in search of drinks.

"I'm calling a breakfast meeting for tomorrow morning. Seven o'clock."

Helen and I groaned.

"What's this all about?" Elizabeth said.

Marni placed her hand on Elizabeth's shoulder. "It's okay, Elizabeth, you can sleep in. It's an editorial meeting."

Elizabeth held her eyes level with Marni's. "I said: what's this all about?"

"Time to crack the whip, I'm afraid. We need to tighten up our schedules, lay out assignments for who's covering what. I want to maximize our time here, justify the expense of sending so many people down."

Brian appeared and handed Elizabeth a drink. "Everything all right?"

Marni's face wore a challenge. "We're just realizing this is probably our last chance at some free time while we're here. So kind of you to invite us, though."

Brian turned to Elizabeth. "I've never thought of you as a taskmaster. Have you changed?"

I watched Marni's face tighten and Elizabeth's eyes go metallic. "Let's all take a look at that schedule together tomorrow," Elizabeth said. "I'm sure we can work it out."

"Then can we move the meeting to seven-thirty at least?" Good old Helen. "The first show tomorrow isn't until nine."

Elizabeth turned to Marni. "I don't think that will be a problem, do you?"

Rage clouded Marni's eyes in the second before she answered. "I'm sure we could all use the extra half-hour sleep." Beat. "Right, Rosemary?"

What? What had *I* done?

I sat on the bed and spooned some Ben & Jerry's ice cream into my mouth. "So Marni's really been on my case today. No let-up since last night."

Brian, wearing only his boxers, was doing push-ups on the floor beside the bed.

"I can't really see what her value is to *Panache*," he said. "Her observations on the collections weren't very astute."

"Is that what you two were talking about at supper last night after the show? That stuff's my job. Her role in life is to be the boss. You know — co-ordinate, unite warring factions, stand up to the business people. She sure has been irritable lately, though. Since Elizabeth hit the scene, in fact. Mega bad mood time. And I don't know why she's treating me like I'm some sort of traitor."

Brian rolled over and started with sit-ups. "Do you think she suspects?"

"About us? Even if she does — which, how could she, when we've been so bloody discreet? — why should she care?" I looked down at his steely abs. "Great ice cream," I said. "Want some?"

He sat up all the way. "I may have to leave New York early. Something's come up in London. I'll know tomorrow morning."

I put down the ice cream. "A simple no thanks would have sufficed."

"I'll leave a message at your hotel. I'll use the name Peter. Okay?"

How about Dick? "Fine," I said. "Be like that."

Chapter Eight

On my way out of the house, early for once, I decided to walk a few blocks over to Fab Food to pick up coffee and a bagel, fuel for my trip downtown. I tried for a brisk stride, pretending not to notice that there was a certain cold dampness in the air — a pre-fall kind of chill. Good thing I was wearing my new silver trench coat. Not that it was technically waterproof, or even warm. But still. It looked good — that should count for something.

Naturally, I hadn't checked the weather forecast before leaving home (when am I ever outside?) nor thought to bring along anything as useful as an umbrella. So when a major downpour suddenly hit, it was only a matter of minutes before my impractical coat was soaked through and my hair's half-hour-long blow-drying job ruined.

By the time I arrived at Fab Food and pulled open the heavy glass door, I was in a semi-hysterical state that I told myself could be repaired only by the immediate downing of an extra-large café au lait. I placed my order, picked out a bagel, stood by the cash, and watched the server perform the espresso ritual. I chewed down my first mouthful of warm carbs and saw in the mirrored wall behind the counter that my hair was completely flat and mascara was smudged in dark watery lines down my cheeks. I groaned and rubbed at the black splotches with a paper napkin.

In mid-eye-wipe, I heard voices coming from the back of the shop. I turned toward the cheese display cases, where I saw a manager type standing, his back to me, talking to someone. Among the towering displays of bottled apricot chutney and bags of taro chips, I spotted flashes of blonde hair and a rust brown suede jacket. Probably a rich young matron arranging a catered lunch in picnic baskets for the drive north to admire the autumn colours.

The espresso machine gurgled and my body twisted, drawn to the sound of the steaming milk like a baby to the breast.

The counter guy pushed the coffee toward me. As I raised the Styrofoam cup to my parched lips, a voice beside me said, "Rosemary! Hi."

The young matron from the back had morphed into my sister Julie, who, though blonde, wealthy, and prone to wearing animal skins, was actually one of the good guys. "Hi, Julie. I didn't recognize you back there. New jacket?"

"Yeah. You like it? It's a present from Don. He was trying to cheer me up."

"Why do you need cheering up?"

"I don't, really. He just thinks that . . . oh, maybe he's right. Maybe I do need a break from planning luncheons."

"Is that what you're doing here? What's this one for?"

"Hospital fund-raising committee."

"Oh."

"I know. My life. What about you? Heading down to the office?"

"No. I'm off to the ready-to-wear collections at the King Edward Hotel. They start today."

The manager guy walked up, smiled, said, "Excuse me," and, to Julie, "The chef suggested we add a salad of pear, watercress, and walnuts. What do you think?"

"Sounds great," I said. "Can I come?"

"It does sound lovely," said Julie. "Max, have you met my sister Rosemary? Rosemary, this is Max Appelbaum. He's the owner here."

I shook hands with Max, who was short and slight and wore glasses, and had reddish hair flecked with grey that stood up straight on his head. And a good handshake. "I always wondered who the Fab in Fab Food was," I said.

"You're Julie's sister?"

"Rosemary's the fashion editor of *Panache* magazine," Julie said proudly.

I wondered why Julie was acting Mom-ish and fixed a plastic smile on my face, waiting for Max to make the typical comment about how Julie and I don't look alike.

"I've seen you in here before," he said. "I didn't know you were related to Julie."

"Yeah, well, the resemblance is all in our elbows." I raised my bent arm and pointed to my elbow, expecting Julie to do the same — it's an old family joke — but she said, "Oh, Rosemary," and, to Max, "She's just kidding."

Max leaned toward me — I leaned back — and touched my face with his finger. "There's a poppyseed on your cheek. There, I got it. Aren't those bagels great?"

I fixed my makeup in the cab, wove the wayward tresses into a French braid, extracted two more poppyseeds from my teeth, and felt almost restored when I walked into the King Edward. That is, until I spotted a ridiculous creature walking up the stairs ahead of me. The red-and-white-striped cotton stovepipe on her head, straight out of *The Cat in the Hat*, was already more than enough. Did she also have to wear leopard-print leggings and a flowered smock top? I ground my teeth. These shows were supposed to be for the trade only — no fashion victims allowed.

I wiped off the warm welcome I received at the registration desk and strolled into the media and buyers' lounge, where I spotted all the usual faces helping themselves to the free fresh-squeezed orange juice and five kinds of tea.

The normal thing to do at this point would have been to relax into the familiar presence of my compadres, but instead I found myself thinking thoughts like: Megan, dear, that long curly hair is so out now, get it cut off, you fool. And: Hey, Josephine, it's about the mini-kilt with the chenille sweater — you think you're supposed to be living trends or buying them? And: You. Over there. In the gold-studded sausage casing. Will you be a fashion *Don't* in my next is-sue?

I walked into the ballroom and took the seat with my name on it in the front row, next to Helen. Helen said Hi, saw my face, and bus-ied herself reading the program. I sat there jiggling my foot and decided I'd be really pissed off if the first show started late, on top of everything. I mean, we weren't in Paris here.

But right on time the lights went down and the speakers shot out a blast of heavy metal music — this at ten o'clock in the morn-ing. Not that any o'clock is suitable for listening to that crap, especially combined with the assault of the three banks of TV lights that switched on in my face. I searched in my bag for my sunglasses, but I'd left them in my coat pocket, and my coat had been checked. My head started aching immediately, no waiting, and I squinted at the first piece, some godawful apronlike jumper item worn by a young model named MouMou (don't ask) who had apparently de-cided that this was not the King Edward Hotel but Schwab's Drugstore, and she was about to be discovered.

So MouMou didn't simply walk or slink — she skipped and hopped and pranced. At the end of the runway, in front of the cam-eras, she paused extra-long so the girl behind her had to double back, then she winked at somebody imaginary across the room and blew a kiss to some other ghost. She turned upstage at last and romped on, apparently unaware of the mortal danger she faced from my rampant homicidal urges.

I kept my facial expression neutral, wrote the words "utter gar-bage" in my notebook, and felt a sudden wave of sickness. In a second, I was drenched with sweat and shivering. I touched my tem-ples, felt the dizziness invade, and closed my eyes against the nausea, and I must have made some sort of moaning noise, because I heard Helen say, from a great distance, "Rosemary, are you all right?"

And then I fainted, right onto the carpet beside the runway.

When I came to, seconds later, the first face I saw, haloed by those infernal lights, was, of all people's, MouMou's. Her cool fingers were pressed against my neck, her head was bent down near mine, and she seemed to be listening. I gazed at her false eyelashes and at a shiny black sequin glued to her powdery cheek. No poppyseeds there. I watched her lipsticked mouth say to Helen, "Could you find a cold wet cloth?"

She sat up and looked into me, examining my eyes, it seemed like. She smiled a beautiful smile. She was a beautiful girl. "I hope Marco doesn't think it was his clothes that made you pass out," she whispered.

I smiled feebly and leaned on the bony arm she offered to help me sit up. Helen appeared with a cloth napkin in hand, and to a scattering of applause, MouMou ambled up onto the runway. Helen led me out of the room and into the washroom, where I made it just in time to evacuate everything I'd eaten or drunk in the preceding twelve hours, starting with the bagel and coffee.

I opened my eyes, instantly wide awake. The bedside clock read 2:04. In the morning. What had woken me? I listened for outdoor sounds but heard no gunning engine, no drunken whooping. I listened for indoor sounds. No water running through pipes, no murmur of my upstairs neighbour's TV. Then I felt the twinge in my abdomen. Wonderful. My stomach had woken me up. Great week I was having. That sudden onset of the flu at the collections two days ago, and now this. I got out of bed and padded into the bathroom.

On the toilet, I barely had time to pull down the underwear and hike up the T-shirt before the shit shot out of me at top speed, which was pretty disgusting, but at least I wasn't throwing up. I hated throwing up.

I sat there. Was it over yet? So much for the flu having been of the twenty-four-hour variety, huh. Unless this bout of sickness was thanks to the Szechwan food I'd had for dinner. And the pot I'd smoked afterwards probably hadn't helped. Another volley, very liquid, with some crampiness in the stomach. I wiped and flushed and waited for more. And almost smiled, thinking how my current symptoms matched those of the illness I'd manufactured for Marni and Carolyn's benefit that time in Paris — the cover story for my first sex session with Brian. Hey. No reminiscing about Brian allowed, remember?

I leaned over and rested my elbows on my knees, my head on my hands. All done now? I felt a stab in the gut, a different kind of pain. I clutched my stomach. The cramp was sharper this time, deeper. My head started doing a very scary slow rev.

I fumbled next to me for the cold water tap and turned it on. I held my hand under the stream of water and tried to splash some on my face, on my eyes. My head was really moving now, and the inside of my face was heating up. I started to cry. My head spun out, I half-screamed, and I fainted.

The tile was cool against my cheek, against my legs. How lovely to be lying down. The little drops of condensation on the floor under my skin felt refreshing. Though I was in a strange position. Face down, legs twisted, lips smooshed against the tile. With great effort, I rolled over onto my back and opened my eyes, looked at the ceiling. The bathroom ceiling. Right. I was lying on the bathroom floor. This was normal.

I sent the tongue around the inside of my mouth. Definitely a taste of blood there. And the feel of a blister. Must have fallen face-first on the floor when I fainted, hit my lips with my teeth. I touched my forehead. Ouch. A bruise there, too. Probably hit the bathtub on the way down. Nice work.

At least I had nowhere else to fall, though. This was good. Yup, lying on the cool floor was where to be. If only that awful rushing noise would stop.

What was that noise, anyway? I listened hard, tried to isolate its location. Eureka. It was the sound of running water from the sink. But there was no way — absolutely not — that I could get up to turn off that tap. I closed my eyes and watched my head zoom in and out. Hold on there, head. And that noise! Like listening to a conch shell in Florida, only louder. Way too loud.

I imagined the phone beside my bed. It wasn't any closer than the tap, but maybe, in a while, I could reach it and call Julie and get her to come over, let herself in with her key, and turn off that water. And look after me. Good idea. I'd have to try that. After the room stopped spinning.

I opened my eyes. The tile was cold now, and my skin was covered with goosebumps. I shivered and my teeth started chattering. Without lifting my head, I reached up, snagged a towel hanging from the rack and let it drop onto my legs. That was better, warmer. But that noise.

How about if I stood up — really fast — and, in one incredibly quick movement, turned off the tap and made a run for the bed? The whole procedure would take about five seconds. I checked my head for dizziness. It felt close to clear. I could do it. I could.

Count to three, then go. One. Two. Three — I pushed myself up, made a grab for the tap, twisted it off, half-ran and half-lunged the ten steps to the bed. And fainted again when I landed.

Dr. Sussman eyed me over her glasses. "Love your suit."

"Thanks. It's Jeff Krauss. He did a nice collection last season of work wardrobe stuff. You should check it out."

"It's gorgeous. I will." She opened my file and scanned the

pages. "Now, let's see. We've determined the fainting's nothing to worry about — your chronic response to pain. We've ruled out pregnancy, your blood's healthy, and Dr. Markel says your bowel looks fine."

"Have you ever had one of those bowel examinations done, by the way? We had quite the laff riot over there in his office, me and Dr. Markel. I recommend it highly for anyone looking for an instant diarrhea cure."

She smiled but didn't look up, kept reading the file. "So . . . any problems lately?"

"No. Nothing for a while now. That four weeks of madness, then nothing."

"Well, I'm sure it was just a particularly stubborn gastrointestinal virus."

"So that's it then?"

"Continue to take it easy with your diet and your workload. And keep up the exercise — you're still doing it?"

I stood up. "Yeah."

"Exercise is a great stress reliever," she said, and came around the desk. "And stress was probably a factor. Were you under any extra pressures when this all began? Had anything upsetting happened?"

She placed a light hand on my shoulder.

Oh, no. Not the old stress cop-out. I glanced at her, about to insist I had no such problem, but I saw such concern and sympathy in her face that I had to turn away.

I picked up my coat. "Anything upsetting happen? You mean, other than the emergence of the schoolgirl look for spring? Listen, the best thing to come out of this was that I missed a whole round of covering the collections."

I made a couple more smart remarks, thanked her, donned the coat, said goodbye, waved cheerily to the receptionist, shut the office door behind me, and felt huge heavy tears well up in my eyes.

What? Why?

I rooted a tissue out of my bag, wiped at my face, and headed down the hallway. What was this crying all about?

I pressed the call button for the elevator. Calm down, kid. Calm down. And think for a minute about the possibility that Dr. Sussman could be right.

I stepped into the elevator. So. Extra pressures, extra pressures. There were none I could really recall. Granted, work had been less than fun lately, what with Marni changing her bitch status from amateur to professional. I wished she'd get over her problem already, whatever it was. But other than that? I tried to think back a month.

August had always been our slow time, and this August hadn't been much different. Unless, of course, you counted the break-up with Brian.

I got off the elevator at ground level and navigated the lobby. I passed an old man shambling along on a walker, looked into the pharmacy entrance at two old women sitting on chairs, their legs splayed under their heavy wool skirts, their swollen ankles stuffed into their orthopedic shoes.

What in hell stresses did I have to complain about?

I escaped out the door to the street and hotfooted my way back to work.

Chapter Nine

In darkest January, Julie called me at work. "About your birthday. We could do a family party at my place with Don and the kids, or we could do lunch, you and me."

"Definitely (b)."

"Okay, let's pick a date. And put it in your book now."

"Is it thirty-two I'm turning, or twelve? I can't quite remember."

"Rosemary."

"Sorry. I'm having one of those days."

A small silence from Julie, during which I realized that lately I was *always* having one of those days. "I thought we'd try that new place out on College near Dovercourt," she said. "Perfecto. Or is that too far for you to go on a workday?"

It *was* a little far, but why shouldn't I take a long lunch once a year? "Sounds great," I said, and wrote down the particulars in my datebook, in pen.

Pen or not, I was late for lunch when the day came. I wouldn't have been, only Marni showed up in my doorway wearing a red Valentino dress she usually hauled out for important meetings with people from outside the office — not how I would have classified the internal budget meeting scheduled for that afternoon.

"Hi, Marni." I pushed my desk drawers shut and slipped out of my shoes.

"Got a minute?" she said.

"Just heading out, actually. Can it wait?"

"No, it can't. I need you to take over the budget meeting at one o'clock. I've been called away. Thanks." She turned to go.

To her back, I said, "Sorry, can't do it."

I pulled on my boots and watched her stop, facing away from me, hand on my doorknob. "Pardon?"

Thump, thump. "I said I can't run your meeting. I'm busy."

She turned back and we had one of our little staring contests. I gave way first when I stood up, put on my coat, and threw my purse over my shoulder.

"I guess there won't be a meeting at all, then," she said.

"Guess not."

"You'd better notify everyone. All the secretaries seem to have disappeared."

I stuck out my tongue at her back, took off my coat, sat down, dialled ten phone extensions, got ten voice-mails, left ten messages. And arrived late at the restaurant for lunch.

I settled back in my chair and surveyed the trendy surroundings — everything purple, mustard, and teal, geometric shapes, polished woods and scuffed metals. "So this is some fabuloso place, huh?"

"You know who recommended we come here, by the way? Max Appelbaum. Remember? The owner of Fab Food."

"Oh, yeah. The little guy. Actually, he served me the other evening when I was picking up dinner after a bad day at the office — crabcakes, I had. They weren't bad, either. Have you tried them?"

"I told him I wanted to take you someplace special for your birthday." She folded and unfolded her napkin. "He seemed quite interested in the topic."

"Which topic? Restaurants, or birthdays?"

"You."

"How come?"

"Wanted to know how old were you turning, where you lived, were you single . . ." She avoided my eye.

"You're not trying to set me up?"

"Maybe."

"Look, I'm sure he's a nice guy and everything, but he's not my type." I pictured Max — his slight build, his soft voice. And I flashed on an image of Brian — those piercing eyes, the curve of his upper arm when his biceps were flexed, the cords in his neck — then wiped the screen clear. "Anyway, I don't do blind dates."

"It wouldn't be blind. You know him already."

"Julie."

"Okay, fine. I'm still glad we came here. It's good to check out new restaurants. Visit other planets."

"Planeto Perfecto?"

"I need to get out of my orbit more."

"Since when did you start speaking in metaphors?"

"Do you ever feel that way, though?" she said. "As if you do the same things every day, see the same people, drive the same route to the same places?"

I picked up a piece of twenty-grain bread from the basket and started buttering. "Not exactly."

"Well, I do. I shop for groceries, prepare dinner, drive the kids to their hockey games, pick them up, help out at school, get the skis waxed, gas up the car, pack for the weekend. I run around but I never go anywhere. I'm like a rat in a maze . . ."

I passed my hand in front of her face. "Julie, are you okay?"

"No, I'm fine. I mean, yes, I'm okay. I'm just . . . oh, never mind. What about you? How's your stomach?"

I swallowed a hunk of bread. "Better. I've been working out regularly, and I haven't had fainting or diarrhea for ages. Plus I try not to mix dope and spicy food."

She smiled. "I can't believe you still smoke at all."

"I don't do it that often. But it's a good thing. Relaxing. You should try it some time — when Don's out on call, after the kids go to bed. Some pot and a bowl of popcorn, a little trash TV, and you'll be one mellow creature. I've got some joints rolled in my purse I could give you right now, if you want."

"Very funny."

"No, really." I pulled open my bag and started digging. "I found this stash the other day when I was searching for change to make a phone call. God knows how long it's been in here, but it should still be good. Now where . . . oh, here it is." I held up a clear plastic film canister containing three skinny joints.

Julie's hand closed over mine, she yanked down my arm, and whispered, "What are you, crazy? Someone might see."

I slipped the container into her purse and whispered back, "You do remember how to inhale, don't you?"

She laughed and her pearl-drop earrings shook. "You kill me."

"I seem to recall, when you were nineteen or twenty, it must have been, 'cause I was around ten, and you, you wore all those hippie clothes — tie-dye, bandannas, bell-bottom jeans, the whole bit. Don't tell me you didn't smoke dope then, too."

"Okay, so maybe I tried it a few times. But my wild period lasted for all of about five minutes. I mean, look at me. Do I look like a party girl?"

"It's never too late, Julie."

Over coffee, I said, "I'm so glad you didn't pull one of those surprise numbers with a cake and singing waiters."

Julie was signing the credit card slip. "Who do you think brought me up? Did you talk to them, by the way?"

"Yeah. They called on my birthday and sang, in harmony and everything. They asked if I'd come down to Florida in February."

"Why don't you? It'd be great for us all to be together."

"I don't know. It's a bad time for me. The fall collections and everything."

She slipped her card back into her wallet. "And you'd see Brian Turnbull at the shows, right?"

"Not necessarily. He doesn't always go."

"How's life without him, anyway?"

"It's not like I was ever truly with him."

"I know." She stood up. "Shall we?"

I followed her to the front of the restaurant and watched her turn the heads of six different men on her way. Good old Julie, voted Best-Looking Girl in high school, three years running. Unlike me. I'd been voted Best Hair. I mean. What good is hair, except to get you mixed up with Australian philanderers with hair fetishes?

We gathered our gear and stood by the restaurant entrance, buttoning up coats and pulling on gloves. The outer door opened to admit a man in a beaver coat and hat, and we were hit with a blast of cold air. The man brushed past us and walked over to the coat check.

Julie stood with her back to the door, her gloved hand on the handle. "See that woman in the corner booth? There, you can look, she's not faced this way. Isn't that your Marni?"

I squinted into the far dark corner and saw, yes, Marni, in her red dress, holding a wine goblet. Her head was bent close to that of a grey-haired man in a suit.

So she'd been called away, had she? To some romantic rendez-vous, it looked like. And they'd picked a nice, faraway place for it, too. The chances of anyone from *Panache*, or from MacKenzie Communications, even, hanging out at lunchtime in Perfecto was beyond remote. Except for a combination of coincidences like Julie's desire to visit other planets and my birthday. "It *is* her," I said. "Let's get out of here."

We walked out into a biting wind. Julie handed a claim check to the valet parking guy.

"Fuck, it's freezing," I said. "Maybe I *will* consider coming to Florida."

Julie took my arm in hers. "I hope so." She steered me over to the window to read a framed newspaper review hanging there. "What a funny place," she said. "Can you believe Greg Smithfield eating here?"

Greg Smithfield was the Canadian billionaire owner of various important British and North American newspapers, a national business celebrity. "Who told you that? Max Appelbaum?"

"No, that was Greg Smithfield who just walked in. The tall man in the beaver coat."

I looked back at the door. "Somehow I never picture big business types caring enough about food to come way out to a place like this."

Julie shrugged. "Maybe he's here for a meeting."

Yeah, like Marni, who'd had to cancel the budget meeting because she'd been called away. The nerve of her, thinking that the personal thing keeping her away from the office was more important than my personal thing. Not that she knew my thing was personal. But she'd certainly implied hers was business. It'd be different if she'd been sitting in Perfecto having a tête-à-tête with some bigshot like Greg Smithfield —

No. Don't tell me. It couldn't be.

Julie removed her arm from mine and handed the valet a tip. Her Range Rover had magically appeared on the street in front of us.

"Can I take you back to the office?" she said.

I grabbed her by both arms. "Look, I know this sounds crazy, but I'll watch the car if you'll go in and see if Greg Smithfield is sitting with Marni. That's all I ask. Just slide in, grab a book of matches, check it out, and come back. Please?"

Julie examined my eyes the same way MouMou had when I'd fainted, checking for dilated pupils, I'd figured out since. Finding mine to be of a regular diameter, she turned without a word and stepped inside the restaurant. I climbed into the car and shivered, despite the warm air being pumped out by the heater. She was back in a minute, taking off the parking brake and pulling her U-turn. "He was. Three of them at the table. How'd you know?"

"I can't believe it."

"What do you think this means?"

I looked out at the frost-whitened street. "That maybe she's interviewing for a job. That maybe she'll get it. That maybe I'll have a shot at being editor."

"Is that what you want?"

I didn't have to think long. "I think I'd rather be doing something completely different."

Julie sighed. "I sure know that feeling."

Chapter Ten

Back at work, I dragged Helen into the coffee room and told her what I'd seen at Perfecto.

"This could be our big chance," Helen said, as we headed back to my office.

"For what?"

"To take over the world. Or at least *Panache*."

She still wanted to? "I don't know, Helen. There's probably an innocent explanation for what I saw. We shouldn't get our hopes up."

"You going to tell Carolyn about Marni?"

"No way. Why?"

"Check your messages. She's been ringing your phone off the hook for the last hour."

"Carolyn? Rosemary. You rang?"

"Yes. I got your message that the budget meeting was cancelled. What was that all about?"

Be careful now. "I don't know. Marni couldn't make it, so she asked me to tell everyone."

"Why couldn't she make it?"

"Who cares? A day without a budget meeting is like a day with sunshine, if you ask me."

"Uh-huh. Listen, Rosemary — just between us — have you noticed Marni acting a little strange lately?"

I sipped my coffee and shrugged at the same time, took some liquid down the wrong way and started coughing. Through the noise of spit-up coffee splattering my desktop, I managed to yell out good-bye and hung up.

She called right back. "Are you okay?"

"I'm fine. Sorry. A little choking fit there."

"Well, seeing as there's no budget meeting, how about we use the time to meet on that washed-silk story?"

What could I say? "Okay, but can you come here? I'll get Helen to sit in. And bring chocolate."

"Pardon?"

"Never mind."

My feet were up on my credenza, my back to the door, and I was saying, "But I think MouMou's look would work for this — she's got that extreme paleness thing down, and the white hair."

"I don't agree," Carolyn said. "We need someone more fragile-looking. There's something too strong about MouMou. You should have seen her that time you fainted at the ready-to-wear, acting like a superhero. Oh, hi, Marni."

Marni stood in my doorway, still in that red dress. I looked her over for signs she'd accepted a juicy job offer while she'd been out, but there was nothing obvious — no flushed cheeks, glittering eyes, or big cheque hanging out of her pocket. "We're talking about the washed silk story," I said to her.

"For April," Helen said.

Marni leaned against the doorframe. "And Carolyn doesn't like Rosemary's choice of model?"

Carolyn shifted in her chair. "From what I've seen, no."

"You're basing this opinion on one incident?"

"I think there are other girls who'd be easier to work with. What do *you* think?"

Marni looked right at me. "If there's one thing I've learned in this business, it's that you can't always believe your eyes. You see something, you think you know what it's all about, and you end up being wrong. Don't you find that, Rosemary?"

I returned her stare, for the second time that day. "Appearances *can* be deceiving."

"My point exactly. But carry on. Rosemary: no problems with cancelling the budget meeting?"

She was out the door. I spoke to her back. "No. I gave everyone the message. About your conflict."

"Thank you." She walked away.

There was a silence during which Helen and I avoided eye contact and Carolyn flipped through her file. "Oh, Helen," she said, "I forgot to bring my datebook. Would you be a sweetheart and pop down to my office for me? It should be on my desk."

Helen looked at me to see if she should, I gave her the sign, and she left the room.

Time for this meeting to end already. "You know what, Carolyn? I don't care who we use. You don't want MouMou, fine."

"Good." Carolyn leaned over and pushed my door shut. "See what I mean about Marni?" she said. "What was with that speech about appearances being deceiving?"

I doodled on my notepad. "I've always been quite partial to that cliché, myself."

Carolyn picked up her pen. "Oh, forget it. Let's finish this up." She began talking logistics. I pretended to listen and wondered what Marni could possibly be up to.

I called Marni when I read her E-mail message. "Listen, Marni, about the rescheduled budget meeting — "

"It's not a meeting. It's a hands-on work session."

"Whatever. But I'm a bit snowed under, and I wondered if — seeing as I've done a budget a few gazillion times before — if maybe I could just, you know, skip this one. Okay?"

One of her deadly pauses. "I need you there, Rosemary. Clear your calendar. You're so well organized, I know that won't be a problem."

The budget session was held at a hotel. Not that we didn't have perfectly good conference rooms at the office, but Marni was lately into bullshit like off-site meetings. So you could concentrate better, or focus more, or maybe think what you were working on was actually meaningful in some way.

But when the appointed morning came, I just felt sleepy. I sat down at my spot in the hotel meeting room, took one look at the brown vinyl blotter, the pristine pad of lined paper, and the two sharpened pencils sitting there, and yawned.

Meanwhile, the assembled meeting accessories seemed to program everyone else into serious mode. Not much chat beforehand, and then during the meeting no one joked at all or threw any gossip into the conversation. There aren't that many ways to have fun in a meeting anyway, but at this shindig — and it had to start at the painful hour of eight a.m. to make it seem truly crucial — fun was definitely not on the agenda.

Marni went on and on about the driest garbage imaginable: the importance of sophisticated estimation techniques, blah, blah blah. "We are really being scrutinized this time round," she said. "We have to justify every cent. Do you understand?"

I understood. I'd heard this before a few times. So maybe the economy was worse now, and Marni's warnings did sound a trifle more severe than usual, but basically it was the same old story, and, more than ever, I couldn't make myself care. So I spent the meeting:

(a) looking at my watch

(b) doodling, which always drove Marni crazy, convinced as she was that if I was doodling I couldn't also be listening, but could I help it if she assumed everyone else had her limitations?

and

(c) trying to catch the eye of Trish, the beauty editor (and only ally I had in the room), when anything particularly pompous was said.

The meeting dragged on forever anyway, and then some hotel staff wheeled in these round tables covered with platters of sandwiches, which were supposed to be gourmet because they were on chalah and rye buns instead of on white and brown sandwich bread, but still contained the same old unadorned tuna and egg salad and grey slices of roast beef, and I knew this was the time when we were supposed to be all sitting around chewing together and team-building, BUT. I was not in the mood. So I skipped out. During the meeting, when some accounting person was giving an explanation about computer modelling using an overhead projector — does anyone else see the irony here? — and I was planning my project work for the week, I realized I'd forgotten a key file folder at my apartment.

So when I left the hotel, I zipped home in a cab, picked up the file, and on the way back to the office I had the driver wait outside Fab Food while I ran in to pick up something half-decent to eat at my desk.

The Max Appelbaum guy was in the open kitchen talking to the cooks, but he waved at me right away. "Hi, there," he said, and I remembered too late that Julie had said he might be interested in me.

"Hi," I said, "How are you? I'm just rushing through — I've got a cab waiting, and I wanted to grab something quickly . . . "

I scanned the array of prepared food laid out under the glass countertop and tried to decide.

He wiped his hands on his apron. "A sandwich? A lunch special? We've got pad thai today." He pointed to the dish. "I could warm it up for you."

Something about the serrated edges on the fresh coriander leaves garnishing the pad thai made my bowel contract in fear. "No, I don't think so. I was hoping for something more soothing." I looked out at the cab and back at the counter.

"I know what would be perfect." He turned around to reach for a dish behind him. And I got that awful feeling like when I'm in a clothing store where a saleswoman totally hangs over me the entire time, then says, "I have the perfect thing for you," and brings out a chartreuse rubber dress.

Max was holding a steaming casserole dish. "How about some boeuf bourguignon? Over a purée of potatoes, squash, and turnips. Just the thing for a cold day like today."

I inhaled the winey aroma and admired the buttery pile of mashed vegetables piled high in a bowl alongside. He was right. It was exactly what I wanted.

He set down the casserole. "Unless you'd prefer some mixed baby greens with raspberry vinaigrette."

"The beef would be lovely, thanks," I said. "With the purée, for sure."

He cracked a smile and dipped a big serving spoon into the bowl.

Helen appeared at my door just after I'd sat down at my desk. I beckoned her in.

"How was the budget meeting?" she said.

"Terrible. They're expecting big-time financial analysis from everyone. Bar graphs and pie charts and wake me up when it's over, will ya?" I took a bite of the stew and potatoes, still warm out of Max's microwave. "Helen, this food is so good, you've got to try some — here, I have a clean spoon in my drawer."

Helen swallowed a spoonful. "Mmm. It *is* good."

"Have some more. The guy gave me tons. So, anyway, yeah, the budget meeting. Not only was I bored to death, I managed to get into one of those arguments with Marni."

"Rosemary, not again. You promised."

"I know. But she was being particularly — " I saw Marni walking down the corridor toward my office. "And here she is now."

Marni stepped in and dropped a big blue binder on my desk. "Hi, Helen. Rosemary, you didn't stay around long enough to pick up the budget procedures manual at the end of the meeting. But I knew you'd want to study it."

"Gee, thanks."

"Something smells good — where'd that come from?"

"I picked it up on the way here."

She still didn't move.

"I'm allergic to hotel food," I said.

Helen hid a smile behind her hand and Marni put on her pissed-off face.

"No, really," I said. "My doctor told me to watch what I eat."

Marni carefully uncrumpled the cellophane cover I'd left on my desktop and read the sticker label. "Fab Food? Up near Summerhill? Not exactly on the way here from the Plaza II."

"Don't worry," I said. "I punched in on the time clock."

Helen said, "I think I hear my phone ringing," and started to rise, but Marni just gave me a look and left.

I picked up my spoon and put it down again. "Is it me," I said to Helen, "or is she on my case?"

"A match made in hell. Just pray something comes out of her meeting with Greg Smithfield."

"It must have been a false alarm. I've never heard anyone more committed to long-term planning."

"Speaking of planning, I need to talk to you about who's doing what while I'm away."

"But that's not till . . ." I opened my datebook and turned a page. "Not next week, already?" I flipped a few more pages. "And the budget's due while you're gone, too. I don't suppose you could postpone?"

"This is my trip to Australia and New Zealand, remember?"

"Oh. Right."

"Look," Helen said, "get me to do stuff now, this week — I'll put in overtime. Just tell me what you need."

"Yeah, yeah."

"By the way, anyone you want me to look up? You know, when I'm in Sydney?"

I gave her my evilest eye.

"Okay, okay," she said, "just checking."

Of course I didn't get it together enough to delegate work to Helen on the budget. So off she went, my workload became even heavier with her away, and the budget file sat there festering. About three days before it was due in to Marni, when I still hadn't done anything more with the file than shift it around from one corner to another on my desk, I ran into Carolyn at the sinks in the washroom. I was washing my hands, and she was doing this teasing action to her hair with a comb.

"How's your budget coming?" she said.

"Oh, well, you know. How about you?"

She put the comb back in her makeup bag and pulled out a mascara wand. "I decided to get mine out of the way. I used that computer model we talked about at the meeting — one of the finance guys helped me set it up, and it worked out really well. Marni even told me it was the best departmental budget she's seen." She stood back and admired her reflection.

"I don't know," I said. "The whole thing sounds like way too much work to me. I think I'll just make up some figures. Why overcomplicate things, right?"

Carolyn zipped up her makeup bag and looked at me. "You have the weirdest sense of humour, Rosemary."

At our next department head meeting, I walked in late, and when I took my place at the table Marni was praising Carolyn's budget submission. "That was solid, thorough work," she said. "I can't overemphasize the importance of the editorial staff proving we have good business sense."

She turned to me. "Hello, Rosemary. Thanks for dropping in."
Not quite dripping with sarcasm, more of a light ooze.

"Glad to be here."

"I wanted to ask you," she said, and I thought I saw a smirk fly
across Carolyn's face, "about your budget. Particularly this figure on
page three, line twelve."

I fumbled with my copy, panic mounting, because not only had
I rushed through all my figures, I had, in fact, done a substantial
amount of faking and coin-flipping, my estimates founded on no
solid logic whatsoever. That is, I'd been bad. I admit it.

I turned pages, trying to find line twelve, page three, and hoping
it was one of the few items I'd based on something close to reality,
when Carolyn said, "Rosemary likes to make up her figures, don't
you, Rosemary?"

Amid the few nervous titters around the table — Carolyn was
joking, right? — I looked up at her, my jaw slack. I couldn't believe
it. Then I saw Marni and got worried. If Carolyn was making me
wonder what I'd ever done to her, Marni seemed about to explode.
Her eyes were fiery, her cheeks flushed — even the tips of her ears
were red.

Maybe I'd been losing perspective lately, but did this situation
really merit rage?

"I . . . I . . . I . . ." I said.

Marni pushed my budget document aside, leaned back in her
chair, and spoke in a very low, very controlled voice. "Some people
around here seem to think that carefully working through the numbers and doing some strategic planning is not important."

Everyone looked at their shoes, though it was pretty obvious she
was talking about me. My body sure recognized the attack, instantly
speeding up the blood flow to a level I was sure would worry Dr.
Sussman.

"Let me explain to everyone, for what I hope is the last time, that
the financials of this magazine are crucial to its future, and to the
future of all of your jobs."

Dead silence. Even Carolyn was cowed.

"Rosemary," Marni said, "You and I can go over your budget in detail later."

"Sure." Not the time for a wisecrack, I had a feeling.

Marni gave me further shit in private, so I apologized, grovelled all over her office, and spent the whole next week working late and doing the budget properly. Lucky for me, Helen returned from her vacation somewhere in there and helped me out.

When the masterpiece was finally complete and cross-checked and proofed and get-it-out-of-my-life-already, I took it in to Marni's office. I held the binder in my hands like a ring-bearer's cushion and did a slow-motion lockstep up to her desk, but she was sitting in front of her computer, head down, working away, and didn't acknowledge my entrance.

I sized up the papers spread around, the clips from competing publications, the unfamiliar-looking draft layouts. I made some noise. "Whoomp. Here it is."

Her eyes stayed on her computer screen. "I'm busy, Rosemary. Can you come back later?"

"I'm delivering my budget."

"Thanks. Drop it on the credenza. I'm on a deadline here."

No deadline I knew of. I set the binder down. "Anything I can help you with?"

Her fingers came off the keyboard and she looked at me for the first time. "Oh. No. Thanks, but no."

"What are you working on?"

"Something for Elizabeth." She gathered up the papers on her desk as if tidying, when we both knew she was hiding them from me. Then she stopped moving things around and gave me the old glare. "If that's all, Rosemary, I said I was busy."

Later that day, after almost everyone had gone home, Helen stuck her head around my door. "How's your disposition?"

I was leaning back in my chair reading *Women's Wear Daily*. "Ready for a diversion."

She held something behind her back which I hoped was a high-fat, high-sodium snack food. "I wasn't sure if I should show you this," she said, "but I decided you'd kill me if I didn't."

She waved a magazine at me and I glimpsed the title: *Australia Today*. She brought it closer and I saw Brian's smiling face beside that of a blonde young woman. The caption read, "Captain of Publishing Industry Docks His Boat At Home."

I felt a tightness in my chest and reached out for the magazine.

"I guess I'll head out," Helen said. "See you tomorrow."

I turned to the inside story and pored over the pictures of Brian and his fiancée. How young she was, and fair, and long-legged, and pretty in that short-haired, Princess Diana kind of way. Virginal-looking, in a flowered dress in one shot, a pink suit in another. A bit stern in riding togs, straddling a big grey horse as she cleared a jump.

He'd warned me. He'd told me during our break-up talk that I'd be hearing about an engagement sooner or later, that I should be prepared, not take it personally.

Kind of like I wasn't supposed to mind when he showed up in the office one day in August, with Carolyn.

There I am, sitting at my desk, shoes off, and luckily it's soon after lunch, so I've recently brushed my teeth and redone the makeup, though god knows what I'm wearing, and *I* know my legs are unshaven under the opaque black tights I'd pulled out of the drawer when the day had dawned cold, despite the calendar.

I'm on the phone making a business call when I look up and see the two of them standing outside my door. Brian looks great, his hair slicked back, his shirt-tie-suit combination elegant and flattering, though more formal than usual, more of a business look than his regular style. Through the glass, I watch Carolyn talk to Brian, watch her gaze up at him, watch him bend down to hear her better because she's doing her trick of speaking too quietly for him to maintain a safe distance. I end my call.

Carolyn leads Brian into my office. I hold on to my desktop and sink down in my chair, trying to reach my shoes with my feet. "Rosemary," Carolyn says, "you remember Brian Turnbull. I'm giving him the grand tour."

I snag my right shoe with my toe and struggle to standing. I offer Brian my hand. "Yeah. Well. Hi. What brings you to town?"

His handshake is firm and strong and has left a little wad of paper in my palm. I close my fingers around it and listen to his reply.

"I was passing through on business. I had some spare time before my flight back, and I remembered Carolyn had offered to show me around."

"Next, the art department," Carolyn says to Brian. And to me, "Bye, Rosemary."

I sink down in my chair, turn my back to the glass wall, open my fingers, and unfold the piece of paper. The note reads:

> R — I only have a half-hour to spare. Meet me on the pavement below at 14:00 — we need to talk.

No signature.

I sigh. This cloak-and-dagger stuff is starting to wear thin. I look at the clock — 1:45. Fifteen whole minutes to check my makeup, brush my hair upside down, and fight my premonition of bad news.

I told my secretary I was going to check out a new fabric designer on King, grabbed my purse, and headed downstairs, where a stretch limo was waiting. I climbed in and sat facing Brian, who seemed intent on staring out the window and avoiding my eye. I leaned over and tapped him on the knee. "So where are we going?"

"Somewhere we can talk. Any suggestions?"

"How about Queen's Quay?" I said to the driver, though the weather wasn't right for enjoying the lakeshore — the day had stayed cool, in that late-August wind-from-the-north way that makes people shake their heads and say that summer's already over.

Brian pressed a button to close the partition between us and the driver. "When'd you get in?" I asked.

He didn't answer, just kept looking out that window.

"How are you?" he said, finally.

"Fine. I mean, pretty crazy. Work is nuts — Marni's acting witchlike, and the usual rumours are flying about changes of management. My only hope is that under a new regime I'll get offered a juicy severance package, and I can leave."

Silence from Brian. Wrong answer, I guess. "Here we are," I said. The driver stopped the car in front of Queen's Quay Terminal.

"Rosie . . ." Brian placed his hand over mine. "I don't know how to tell you this. I don't want you to misunderstand."

I knew it. "Let's get out and walk, okay?"

I opened the car door and stepped out and smelled the soothing, familiar scent of rotting algae.

"I'm getting married," he said.

"What, bigamy now?"

"What I mean is, I'm getting divorced from Sarah — "

Unbelievable — he'd uttered her name in my presence for the first time ever.

" — and then, later, I'm marrying someone else."

My mouth hung open.

"Her name is Chloe."

"Chloe? Her name is Chloe? How old is she? No adult's named Chloe. What is she? Six?"

He had the grace to blush. "Twenty-two."

Seagulls cried and swooped around us. I started walking toward the water, and he followed.

"Maybe if you started at the beginning," I said, "this would be easier to understand."

Sarah's father had been one of Brian's original backers in his first magazine. They'd married, Brian said, more because they suited each other than for love. And they made a perfect couple — he the rising star, she the vivacious, socially useful wife. After a few years of the glamourous life, they'd agreed not to have children — too much of a bother, too limiting — and to open up their marriage, to see other people. Discreetly, of course.

The affair with me having been one in a series of fun, friendly, no-commitment affairs.

"A girl in every port?" I said. "Was that the general idea?"

He ignored me and went on. About how he met Chloe, a young English show jumper, when she came out to Australia to compete in an event one of Brian's magazines sponsored. They'd fallen in love. "She's very sweet," Brian said. "She wants to give up jumping, breed horses in the country, have a houseful of children . . . and look after me."

His expression during that last bit was plaintive. And made him look every one of his forty-five years.

"Don't you find there's a generation gap?" I said.

His face closed. "Let's not discuss Chloe further."

"What am I supposed to say? Thanks for trading me in?"

"You're not the type to settle down."

A red mist had formed behind my eyes and was pressing down on the flood of tears already gathering there. "You know dick about what type I am."

He stopped walking and held out his arms, and, fool that I was, I collapsed into them. "Poor Rosie," he said, "I never meant to hurt you."

I sniffled into his chest and blinked a few times, hoping a salty tear would splash onto the silk of his tie and stain it, permanently.

We sat down on a bench overlooking the water. "Look," he said, "this was never supposed to . . . I *am* sorry."

I crossed my arms in front of me. Damn right he should be sorry. Because, well, because he was dumping me, of course. Not that he'd ever misled me, come to think of it. He hadn't made promises, nor had he claimed exclusivity. And if I'd let my mind wander in that direction once or twice, late at night, if I'd occasionally unlocked the door on the happily-ever-after fantasy when I well knew that gateway should be firmly barred . . . okay, I was a total idiot.

"I'm tempted to suggest one final fling," he said. "But I suppose it wouldn't be right."

So it was like that, was it? What a cad. Pity the poor girl who was going to expect fidelity from this rover. And pity the pathetic woman who considered the one last fling concept for even a second. Considered it, that is, until I conjured up the unseemly vision of me, lying naked in his bedsheets after he'd gone, feeling like a piece of dirt and crying.

I stood up. "No, it wouldn't be right."

We walked some more. A foghorn sounded nearby. I blew my nose. "Does she have to be so WASPy, though?"

"It's not like that," he said. "One day you'll understand."

Now where had I heard that line before, once or twice? It had been one of my mom's favourites, I seemed to recall, used on occasions like the time she found me sobbing my eyes out in my bedroom one day when I was in grade seven and had coaxed me into telling her what was wrong.

She'd hugged me close to her when I'd blurted out the awful truth: that Stephen Macaulay had asked my best friend to the dance instead of asking me.

"Oh, sweetheart," she said, "there'll be other boys who appreciate you. Boys who'll love *you* the best."

I buried my head in her shoulder. "But don't you see? He doesn't like me because I'm . . ."

I knew somehow I couldn't say what I really thought, that he hadn't picked me because I was half-Vietnamese, because he'd be embarrassed to have my visible-minority face at his side at the dance in front of all his fair-haired friends.

So I said, "Because I'm adopted."

Poor Mom. Probably broke her heart clean in two.

Mom had hugged me harder. "It's not that," she said. "You'll see. One day you'll understand."

And one day your prince will come. Believe in fairy tales like that and look where you end up.

I shut *Australian Life* and started putting away the papers on my desk. So the world doesn't change. So I was doomed to continually relive the disappointments of childhood. Time to get over it. Five months had passed now since Brian had given me the kiss-off, and I'd already spent the required number of self-pitying evenings in my apartment listening to Bonnie Raitt sing the blues. Plus my body had done its bit with all that fainting and diarrhea.

Hell, I'd even been able to come around to the point where I could admit that Brian had been right. I didn't want to marry him and live in country isolation, being the brood mare while he donned the nice clothes and went off to the city making deals, doing the fun stuff. No way.

I knew all this, but I sat there for a while in my office and stared out at the darkened desks and cubicles and the flying toasters on the computer screens. The thought of dragging myself out the door one more time up to the health club, over to the designer pizza take-out place, and home to my apartment and my VCR was pretty depressing. And the thought of repeating today tomorrow, and the day after that, was more than I could bear.

I turned the pages of my datebook, looking at the days and weeks ahead. It was impossible, of course, to think of getting away, especially with the fall collections coming up. Unless I talked Helen into covering for me, heavy. Which might work if I offered to send her to Europe in my place.

Of course, I'd have to clear that with Marni, but the way we'd been getting along lately, she'd be ecstatic not to travel with me.

I picked up the phone and dialled Air Canada. "I'd like to check flight times for Toronto-Miami, please."

Chapter Eleven

I hadn't been able to book a seat to Miami on the same day as Julie and her gang, so I was flying down a few days ahead.

The night before I left, I called her. "Hi, it's me, I — "

"Just a second. Smoky! Put that shoe down now! Bad dog. Sorry, Rosemary. I'm going nuts here. I don't know why I do these things."

"What things?"

"Go on vacation. It's more work for me than staying home. The laundry, the packing, making all the stupid arrangements for the house beforehand. And why? So I can spend a week down in Florida looking after the kids full time with zero solitude. And then I get to come back and unpack and launder and replenish the household supplies for another week."

"And people wonder why I'm single."

Julie laughed. "I know how I must sound. Never mind. Why'd you call?"

"Just to say — "

"Grahame! Stop that right now! How many times do I have to tell you? I'm sorry, Rosemary. I'd better call you back."

"Never mind. It was nothing. See you down there."

I'd brought *Vogue* and *Elle* and *Mirabella* to read on the plane, but somehow I just couldn't do more than flip through and throw them into my carry-on bag for later, much later. This was supposed to be my vacation. So I reclined my seat and tried to get into the holiday spirit.

I should mention that, in keeping with hot trends for spring, I was wearing beige linen trousers, a matching cropped jacket, Jack Purcell canvas tennis shoes, and a blush pink T-shirt. Which made me stick out among the vacationing families like, well, like a banana in a basket full of white bread. No one else on the plane seemed to care what was current. Those not in sweats and sneakers wore jeans with denim shirts and cowboy shoes, having not heeded *Panache's* recent declaration that Western-style footwear was categorically "out."

I stood up to go the washroom and noticed some of the better-dressed women — the ones whose denim shirts were pressed and had embroidered Southwestern motifs on them — giving me the twice-over as I made my way down the aisle. And were they thinking, Wow, is that babe ever in style? Doubtful. It was more like they were elbowing the husband and whispering, Hey, honey, get a load of that crazy get-up. I closed the washroom door behind me, checked my reflection in the dull mirror, and resolved to do some shopping in Miami, in a mall. Maybe if I bought some real-person clothes, I might turn into one.

I staggered into my parents' condo with my bags, hugged my mom extra-long, and was dismayed to find a lump forming in my throat at the feel of her spongy chest pressed against mine.

She had Earl Grey tea and currant scones waiting for me. "Dad should be back from golf soon," she said. "Time enough for us to have a nice cup of tea and a chat. You look pale, dear, are you tired?"

I sank into a kitchen chair, felt a warm breeze ruffle my hair from the wide-open balcony doors, and let my eyes rest on the expanse of blue sky out the window. "This is so peaceful, Mom. I'm glad I came."

She set the teapot on the table and sat down. "And I'm glad you're here. How's everything at work?"

"Fine. Well, not great. I'm getting a bit fed up, to tell the truth."

"Do you want to talk about it?"

I smiled. "Not really."

"All right. And what about your social life? Any news there?"

"No news except bad news, but that's okay." I poured myself some tea.

"It's that Australian fellow, isn't it?"

Uh-oh. I'd never told her about Brian. I hadn't thought she'd be too understanding of the married-man aspect, the casual nature of our sex. "How did you — ?"

"Has he gone back to his wife?"

"Not exactly." I explained about the divorce, the new fiancée. "How'd you know about him, anyway?"

She stood up and started rearranging the scones on a plate at the counter. "We forced Julie to tell us. She didn't want to. But it had been so long since you'd had a boyfriend. And all those fashion people are so wild. The clubs, and the tattoos, and I've been reading about the body piercing — " I laughed here, but she went on, "and I can only imagine the drugs. So we asked Julie what was going on, and she said not to worry, it was only a married man." She sat down and placed the plate of scones on the table.

"Oh, Mom."

"You're better off without him, you know, two-timing swine. And you mustn't mind that Julie told."

I reached for a scone. "You're right. I don't mind. What are big sisters for?"

Mom shook her head. "I worry about her, too."

"Why? What's wrong?"

"She hasn't told you?"

"No."

"She hasn't said anything specific, but she seems unhappy."

"What does she have to be unhappy about? With her perfect body, perfect life?"

Mom frowned. "Is that what you think? Did you know she's started painting furniture again?"

"What do you mean, again?"

But then Dad came in and wanted to know about the flight and my rental car and the weather in Toronto, and it wasn't until sometime later that I remembered to ask Mom what the story was on Julie and the furniture painting.

Since kindergarten, my mother told me, Julie had showed a knack for drawing and painting, had always liked art, but it had only been a hobby, a footnote on her high-achieving résumé. That is, until the year she graduated with her BA in political science and economics.

Julie, who had always taken the high road, Julie the good, obedient daughter, had balked at entering law school. She'd planned her career well in advance, had been accepted, no problem, but had surprised Mom and Dad by announcing she was going to take some time off first, get a job.

"What's wrong with that?" I asked Mom.

"Nothing, of course, we know that now. But at the time, we worried. Don't forget, this was back in 1974, hippie days."

Julie had been pretty straight in high school, I remembered. She was the cheerleader in sweater sets and pink lipstick and flipped-up hair and madras Bermuda shorts. And when it was time for university, she picked Queen's, in Kingston — land of the preps. She even belonged to a sorority, gag me.

And when some enterprising sorority sister organized a craft show to raise money for a good cause, you could have expected Julie to be right in there, helping out, setting up tables, providing change and extra chairs for the artisans and the junk purveyors and the little old ladies with their crocheted doilies. But you wouldn't have expected her to become friendly with a group of long-haired hippie artists from Toronto, whose craft thing was hand-painted furniture — salvaged wooden pieces that they painted with rainbows and stars and moons and signs of the zodiac. Mom and Dad were sure surprised, anyway.

"The main person in the group," Mom said, "the leader, I suppose you could call him, was rather unkempt, but something about him appealed to Julie. Something Dad and I couldn't understand."

I had a feeling I would have figured it out, though, if they'd have let me meet him. Even at age eleven or twelve, whatever I'd been.

"Now what was his name again?" said my mother. "I can't remember. Something French. Maybe Benoit? Or was it Philippe?"

Anyway, this Benoit-Philippe not only had bedroom eyes — I'm guessing here — but had something else besides, a certain touch, a little talent, and Julie discerned it, was drawn to the glimmer of beauty on a painted bookshelf.

I could see it all. Julie hanging out at the Queen's craft show and being invited to come down to Toronto some time, visit the group's "space" — a dirty communal loft in a seedy waterfront warehouse. I could see Julie coming home for the weekend, letting her long wavy hair dry naturally instead of setting it in rollers, finding something not pink or plaid to wear, and heading downtown. And when she finished at Queen's and came home for the summer, she stood in our parents' kitchen, Birkenstocks on her feet and a bandanna in her hair, smoking cigarettes and telling them she was not going to law school, and she was not going to be living at home, either.

I touched Mom's soft arm. "You're talking about Julie now, the same one I know. My sister."

"You don't remember any of this?"

No, I didn't. Why not? Had they kept it from me? Maybe. Partly. Not anymore, though.

Now Mom was telling me there'd been major battles, but Julie had won, in the end — how could Mom and Dad stop her? She'd moved out and into the loft and gotten a waitress job, or rather a counter help position at a groovy basement cafe that served alfalfa sprout sandwiches and herbal tea.

And when she wasn't working, she was driving around with Benoit-Philippe in his van, picking up furniture from the roadside left out for garbage, haunting the Salvation Army, becoming garage-sale regulars.

She went on like this for a year and a half — waitressing, salvaging, painting. Mom and Dad made a peace of sorts with her, and she attended family functions — another reason I hadn't noticed this period as being different. She still showed up for birthdays, Christmas, and Thanksgiving. So maybe her hair was less done, was tied up with batiked scarves, maybe she'd replaced her plaid pants with paint-stained overalls — I just thought she'd updated her look to reflect what was cool.

"So what happened? What made her climb back on the straight and narrow?"

"Her boyfriend left."

He'd taken off one day, suddenly. The loftmates had come home and found him and his possessions gone. He'd left a jaunty note saying he'd gone to New York, no forwarding address. And the collective had fallen apart. No one was motivated or organized enough to keep the place together, except, of course, Julie, who could have done it but didn't want to without Benoit-Philippe.

My parents had seized their moment.

"I wonder now," Mom said. "What if we hadn't helped her then, found her an apartment? What if we hadn't encouraged her to start law school the next fall? Maybe we did the wrong thing."

"Come on, Mom. Maybe she's a little depressed right now, maybe her life seems a bit routine, but you don't think she wishes she'd stayed a penniless craftsperson, do you? Versus ending up Julie Jamieson, mistress of house, chalet, and cottage?"

Mom gave me a stern look. "All I know is that she's started painting again. And she hasn't been her usual self." More gently, she said, "You're not the only one who has problems."

A few days later, I went to meet Julie and her brood at the airport.

Grahame, age seven, said Hi, allowed me to hug him, and asked if there was a video arcade in the airport. Taylor, thirteen and already too cool to embrace an aunt, gave me a high five. I gave it back and checked out the bandanna he wore over his shoulder-length hair, the gold stud in his newly pierced ear, the leather cord bracelets around his wrist.

Don waved hello and went off in search of the luggage. Julie kissed me, thanked me for coming, said, "You look . . ."

"What?" I was wearing my purchases from the mall, the type of outfit everybody wore in Florida: faded jean shorts, a faded T-shirt, and my Jack Purcells.

"Summery. You look summery." Her voice turned sharp. "Grahame, don't run off!"

We struggled out of the terminal with their ten bags, and I said to Julie, aside, "So, Mom and Dad and I can keep them entertained for a few hours. Take it easy, don't come back until dinner time, try out the bed in your condo." I nudged her and winked.

"I don't think so," Julie said, without a trace of a smile.

I adjusted the shoulder strap of the bag I was carrying. "If you'd rather I didn't . . ."

"No, I'm sorry. You know what family travel is like. It brings out the worst in everyone." She closed her eyes for a few seconds, then opened them. "Sure, thanks, that would be a help."

The next morning, I dropped by Julie's for breakfast. Don had already left for the golf course, the kids were sleeping in after our late dinner at a steakhouse, and the apartment was quiet. She poured coffee, I unwrapped some of Mom's fresh-baked cinnamon rolls, and we sat out on the balcony overlooking the beach, watching the weather move across the sky and the old people walk along the shore in ones and twos.

"You didn't say much at dinner last night," I said.

"I was tired."

I gestured toward the boys' bedroom. "They getting to you?"

There'd been a few words the night before with Grahame, who wouldn't try the spinach salad, said he hated beef, and announced he would only eat fish and chips, though fish was not on the menu (his dinner had consisted of french fries and a chocolate milkshake). Then when Taylor had been asked to turn off his Walkman at the dinner table, he'd said, in the loud way people talk when wearing earphones, "You don't expect me to listen to your stupid conversation, do you?"

Julie avoided my eye. "You want to know the truth? Look, I love the kids, and Don and I get along fine, but I wish — god, it sounds too awful, but here it is — I wish the three of them could have come down here and I could have stayed home by myself. There, I said it."

I handed her a cinnamon roll. "You want some time alone? That's normal. I'm always craving time alone."

"But you have a job, you work long hours. Whenever I complain to Don, he says I'm spoiled, that I have huge chunks of time to myself when the kids are at school, while he has to be at the office or on call. He never gets any time off except here. This is his idea of a vacation, getting away from Toronto, from his patients, his beeper — getting away and playing golf.

"Of course he's right — it *is* different — I do have most of a day, every day. I just feel so trapped by having to pick up milk and arrange something for dinner, and pack Grahame's knapsack for school and sign the kids up for soccer and tidy the house for the cleaning lady. Oh god, I sound like such a rich bitch, it's too disgusting."

"Have you considered going back to work?"

"It's occurred to me. Not as a lawyer, for sure. Too much bullshit. But volunteer work isn't doing it for me, either. I can't stand those committees for much longer, women sitting around all day talking about where to buy centrepieces for their holiday tables and

Do you know a good plumber? It's enough to make me turn to drugs."
She smiled at this last bit to show she was exaggerating a little.

"God, Julie, here I thought you lived for that stuff — decorating your house for Christmas, those ladies' teas. The things I don't know about you — Mom just told me the other day about your secret hippie past, handpainting furniture."

"Did she tell you I bought an old dresser at a flea market out in the country? It's a total piece of junk, but I hauled it into the city and I've been working on it in my basement. When I have time. It's been fun."

She picked some pecans off her cinnamon bun and popped one in her mouth. "You know, it was you who got me started again on furniture painting."

"Me? How?"

"Remember that joint you gave me at your birthday lunch?"

I laughed. "Okay, let's hear this."

She'd found herself alone one weekend day at the ski chalet. She'd pulled a muscle on Saturday and couldn't ski Sunday, so she had sent the boys and Don out, intending to bake some cookies, whip up a cassoulet for dinner.

She'd been searching in her purse for lip balm when she found the film canister containing the joints. She lifted off the lid and sniffed the faint odour of the pot. She picked up a joint and held it in her fingers, amazed at how familiar it felt. Well, why not? The others wouldn't be back for hours, and if it got scary she could just lie down. She hadn't been sleeping that well anyway. Maybe the dope would help her nap.

"So? Did you get a buzz?"

Julie looked around and lowered her voice, but there was laughter in it. "I did, indeed, not a huge one, but enough to make me remember the times when I smoked dope for real, back when I was doing that crazy commune thing downtown with Philippe."

Julie had lain on the Black Watch tartan couch in her chalet, a matching cashmere throw at her feet, Smoky dozing on the floor beside her, and had time-tripped back to the old days, to the alternative art gallery openings, the lentil stews, the dances on Ward's Island, and to "this incredible painting I did on a huge armoire — well, it seemed incredible at the time. It was probably quite awful, but I haven't thought about it for ages, I could barely remember what it looked like, and when I was lying there on the couch, almost asleep, it came back to me. I saw it so clearly — a whole Lord of the Rings panorama — I know that sounds horribly dated, but it showed the elf forest and the elves and the hobbits and the rings, and, in my mind at least, it looked magical."

So did she. Look magical. Ten years had vanished from her face.

Julie looked into the apartment. "Did you hear something?"

"No. So what? Want more dope?"

She stood up and slid open the screen door. "I definitely heard something."

I looked through the opening and saw a sleepy Grahame, wearing a T-shirt and underpants, come into the living room. "Mommy? I woke up and I didn't know where I was."

"Come have a cuddle, my darling," Julie said, and enfolded him in her arms. The magic had gone from her face, leaving only the lines of motherhood.

It wasn't until a few days later that Julie and I had another chance to really talk. Mom and Dad had offered to take the kids to the Fort Lauderdale science museum, Don was going golfing with the pro from Dad's club, and Julie and I decided to go sailing — my idea — in a rented Shark out of Biscayne Bay.

The wind was light but steady, so we decided on a short sail — a few hours, with time to take turns eating a picnic lunch our mom had packed of cold meat pies, a watercress salad, and lemonade. We navigated out of the marina and away from the heavy water traffic, and Julie picked out a straightforward course. When the way looked clear, I moved to the front of the cockpit and put my feet up, leaned back. "I want to talk more about your furniture painting," I said.

"You don't know how being here doing the supermom thing makes me itch to go home and work on it."

"So this dresser you're working on now, what's it going to be? Another fantasy scene?"

"God, no. I was definitely thinking abstract — lots of vibrant colours. A little zany, busy."

"Kind of a representation of your life right now?"

"Yeah, that's me all right, totally zany. And too busy to ever finish the damn thing."

"You'll finish it."

"The only things I ever get done are time-filling tasks like having dinner parties and helping organize the school fundraiser. Unlike you."

"Yeah, right. Me, I do meaningful shit daily, deciding whether to describe the season's colours as sherbet shades or tropical brights. Quite the accomplishment."

Julie glanced over at me, at my grey Gap T-shirt and grey sweat shorts. "Are tropical brights really in now?"

"Well, no, beige is the big thing. 'Shades of Linen,' our main story for April is called — not my choice of words. Why?"

"Usually I take one look at you and see next season's trend. But you've been dressing differently this trip."

I looked at her outfit: white denim shorts and a cornflower blue T-shirt. No beige in sight, but she looked great. She had that classic thing, always had.

"I'm trying on a new style persona," I said. "Ordinary."

Julie made a noise that would have been a snort on anyone else. "You couldn't be ordinary if you tried."

We sailed on while I wondered why I felt stung by her words, while I gazed out at the shiny water and felt the wind against my cheek.

Julie spoke. "Pretty clear seas ahead. Want to eat?"

"You go ahead. I'll take the helm."

She unpacked the lunch and drank some lemonade from the thermos. "Let's play a game. Name some happy times."

"Huh?"

"I'll start. Happy time number one: getting high with Philippe and staying up all night painting furniture. Happy time number two: winning the gold cup at the RCYC regatta in 1970." She took a bite of meat pie and wiped her mouth with a cloth napkin. "Now you."

Into my mind had popped a picture of Brian and me making love at the George V in Paris. But that didn't seem to qualify. I thought some more. "The first time my name appeared on the *Panache* masthead."

"When was this?"

"'86, I think."

Julie nodded. "Okay, more."

"When I won the Academic Achievement prize at my high school graduation and beat out that nauseatingly perky head cheerleader Beth Pascoe. Your turn."

Julie's smile was wicked. "Becoming head cheerleader." She held up a forkful of watercress. "Going to the Greek islands for the summer after high school and having a fling on Hydra with a young Greek fisherman."

"What's this story?"

Her mouth was full. "You go."

I heard the noise of an engine overhead and looked up to see a small plane towing a banner advertising ladies' night at a local bar.

"You know what I remember?" I said, after a while. "I remember one time when I was about twelve or thirteen, and it was a dull winter day, or rainy — depressing, anyway — and I was at home with nothing to do, and Mom took me to a movie. And she must have taken me to a repertory theatre, because the movie was *Silk Stockings* with Fred Astaire and Cyd Charisse — from the fifties — but on the big screen. And I remember sitting in that theatre, enthralled. Absolutely in love with the idea of Cyd being seduced by Paris, and that long ballet scene where she discovers lingerie, and the two of them dancing in his hotel suite. . . . It was so romantic I thought I'd die."

Julie motioned to me to change places. "Oh, by the way, remember Max Appelbaum? He's seeing a woman now who supplies the store with wild mushrooms. So you're off the hook."

"Oh, good. I can go back there. I was starting to miss the scalloped potatoes."

I ate, we sailed on, and we chatted about nothing. When I'd finished and packed up the cooler bag, I said, "What about the game? I think it was your turn. Or have we run out of happy times already?"

"You know something?" she said. "We've got to change our lives." She gathered up the mainsail sheet in her hand and looked behind her. "And we'd better head back or we'll be out till dinnertime. Ready about."

I released the jib sheet from its cleat and half-stood, prepared to change over.

"About we go," she said, and turned us around.

Chapter Twelve

My first day back at the office after Florida, and I'm standing in line at the Coffee Cup at eight-fifteen in the morning, thoroughly pissed off that the three people in front of me have ordered cappuccinos. With chocolate or cinnamon on top? asks the server-woman, who cannot seem to figure out that she needn't stand stock-still both to ask this question and to wait for the answer. If, instead, she would use the brain in her head to figure out that she can talk, listen, and make cappuccinos *all at the same time*, think of the minutes she would save, think of how customer satisfaction would increase — especially the satisfaction of those customers standing behind the assholes who order cappuccino in the morning, those of us with sophisticated yet simple tastes who would like to purchase their basic extra-large coffee and get the hell out.

You know what? says the first person in line, I think I'd like to try a little of both today — cocoa *and* cinnamon. And the second one says, That sounds nice, I'll try that, too! But the third one can't decide and stands there hemming and hawing while the server still has not moved a muscle, and I am about to leap over the counter and turn on the machine myself when the strength of my feeling becomes sufficient to cross the telepathic void.

"I'll start making them now," the server says generously, "and then you can decide."

She fills the little cup thing with the ground coffee, and I look at my watch for the tenth time in thirty seconds, and I am so tempted, so bloody close to slamming down my empty cup and flouncing out of there, except it will just mean standing in another line-up down the hall for worse coffee. So I simmer and bubble and wait, knowing that cappuccinos take forever to make, even if you're good at getting the milk heated, at swirling the steam spout in the milk at precisely the right angle to make it foam up, nice and thick. Which this Coffee Cup woman is not. Good at it.

Where's the regular guy? My man, my hero. Michael, who is always there in the morning, who only has to glance at me and, without a word, take my cup and fill it with Colombian extra-caf to the right level so I can pour in the large amount of milk I use and not have the thing overflow.

What feels like hours later, I stagger to the elevator, almost finished off by the coffee incident — good thing the cheese biscuit place was a quick, stress-free experience this a.m. and the elevator is uncrowded. Maybe things are looking up.

Except that when I get off the elevator at *Panache*'s floor I must pass Sandy, the receptionist. Torture enough I have to see those shiny red mini-surfboards she wears on the tips of her fingers and find myself imagining — my skin shrinking in horror — what it would be like to be touched by those nails, but does she also have to be so cheery? Practically singing "Good morning" and making the kind of eye contact that communicates with crystal clarity what will happen if I don't respond in like tone and manner. Yes, it's more than obvious that if I don't chirp good morning back at her, whispered charges will be spread through the office during Sandy's break that I am an unfriendly uptight snob bitch who can't utter a pleasant good morning to a person making a quarter of my salary.

In my office, I sit down, take the lid off the coffee, knock it slightly with my hand by mistake, and watch overflow slosh down the sides of the cup. "Shit," I say loudly. I run to the washroom for paper towel and am wiping up the spill when Helen sticks her head around the door and says, "Hi. How was Florida?"

"Fine." It comes out awfully terse. I eye the waxed paper bag containing my buttered biscuit. The biscuit is still warm, but not for long, goddamn it, not for long.

Helen hangs onto the door frame and waits a beat. "Maybe I'll come back later. Would ten be okay?"

I love Helen. "Ten would be fine."

By ten, I'd skimmed through my mail, both electronic and paper, and become less grumpy but more depressed. There had been a long report from Carolyn on graphic design trends in international fashion magazines. I read the summary, skimmed through the rest, and hated everything in it. It reminded me too much of all the ambitious projects I'd planned but not begun, the nonessential items on my project list that had been there for weeks now, inactive. Where did Carolyn find the energy, the drive, the desire?

Helen looked a little apprehensive when she walked through my door at 10:01. "Is this still a good time?"

I waved her in. "Sorry to be a grump this morning. This is why I never take vacations: it's too hard to come back afterwards."

Helen sat down and placed several files on my desktop. "Where should I start?"

"With gossip, of course. Anything juicy?"

"Well, Marni was hidden away all week working on that special project for Elizabeth Crowley."

"Did you find out what it is?"

"No, but Carolyn keeps covering stuff up every time I walk into her office."

"In her case, we can only hope she's working on her résumé."

Helen shrugged. "Other than that, no juice. I wrote down all the boring stuff, here's a status update on our projects and a list of next steps. So can I go to Europe now?"

I read the top line on the status report. "How'd it go co-ordinating the Milan shoot?"

"It was complicated, but between Marni and me, we got it straightened out."

"I guess I'm pretty dispensable, huh."

"Listen," Helen said, "how about some tips on handling Marni in Europe?"

Oh my god, she was humouring me. I was the one who needed tips — she seemed to get along fine with Marni. "Here's my tip:

when in doubt, give her the aisle seat. So, are you all packed? When
do you leave?"

"Four more hours in the office."

And she actually looked excited.

With Helen and Marni away, work went slowly. I attended a studio
shoot for summer officewear and let Carolyn walk all over me. I
tried grousing with Trish, the beauty editor, but she was going
through some personal love problems and wasn't in the mood. I
tinkered with my résumé and tried to make a list of where to send it,
but the only places I could think of seemed no better than *Panache*.

So I was sitting at my desk one day, wondering if it was too late
to go back to school and study something useful, like maybe hair-
styling, when my phone screen lit up with the number zero. Oh boy.
A call from my pal Sandy. "Package here for you," she said and
clicked off.

At reception, she handed me a turquoise gift bag tied with green
ribbon. "Somebody's birthday?" she asked, all twinkly.

I recognized Julie's handwriting on the card envelope. "It's probably a promotional thing," I lied. I carried the bag to my office,
closed the door, opened the card and read:

> *Rosemary,*
> *I saw this and thought of you.*
> *Love,*
> *Julie*

I pushed past the tissue paper and pulled out a framed 8x10
black-and-white photograph of Fred Astaire, dressed in a white
shirt, white pleated pants, a striped tie worn as a belt, an ascot at his
throat, white bucks on his feet. He was dancing, of course — leap-
ing through the air, his body transcribing a graceful arc.

I turned to the wall behind my desk and unhooked a framed *Panache* cover, my first as fashion editor. I hung the picture on the hook and stood back to admire the effect. It looked good, but it kind of put all the tacky stuff on my wall to shame.

A couple of days later, Elizabeth Crowley summoned me to her office. I wondered why, but I came, I sat, and I checked out her Museum of Modern Art desk accessories.

"How about this awful weather?" she said.

I smiled a fake smile. "I hear it's nice in Europe."

"But you decided not to go this season."

"I thought I might have a better perspective from a distance. And Helen can handle it, no problem."

"Ah, yes, your Siamese twin." She made quotation marks in the air with her fingers.

I felt something like gorge rising, though it was probably just that morning's cheese biscuit. "Pardon?"

"You haven't heard you and Helen referred to as the Siamese twins?"

"Seen anyone walking around with a black eye?"

"Rise above, Rosemary. You must rise above these trivialities if you want to get anywhere."

I said nothing. This was getting weird.

"*Do* you want to get somewhere?"

"Gee, *Vogue* offered me the editor's job last week, but I turned it down. New York is just so noisy."

No smile. She picked up a file folder on her desk, and opened it. "I understand you have a journalism degree. And your record with *Panache* is impressive — those national magazine awards are a good stepping stone." She closed the file. "I'm also told you're bright."

By whom?

"I wonder if you'd work on a small project for me."

Like I could say no. "Sure. What is it?"

"I want you to generate some new ideas. Let your imagination run riot. Pretend for a few days that you've been commissioned to relaunch *Panache* — editorial, design, everything. What would you do? What changes would you make? What's your ideal format and content? What kind of pieces would you run?"

She went on, elaborating on the basic concept, while in my mind archived ideas started popping out of their file folders — old story concepts Marni had turned down, articles I'd suggested to the articles editor and never heard of again, dreams I'd built about how different everything would be if I were God.

Not to mention great things I'd seen elsewhere and hadn't tried to steal because I knew they'd never fly at MacKenzie Communications.

Oh, yeah. The incredibly limiting house style of MacKenzie Communications. The departure of Campbell Cameron had really loosened things up — every model didn't have to be blonde, busty and young anymore. Now it was only two out of three.

"Are we talking total blue sky here?" I said. "Am I working within house policy in this fantasy publication?"

Elizabeth thought about that for a minute. "Tell you what. Assume no restrictions whatsoever and see what happens. Okay?"

I asked her more questions. Like what format she wanted, what length, how much detail, and when she wanted it. After she'd spelled it all out, or, rather, said it was mostly up to me but my regular work shouldn't suffer and she wanted something meaty within ten days, I said, "Can I ask what this is all about?"

"Just a brainstorming exercise. I like to do this now and then to keep the creative juices flowing. I've found it to be quite rewarding in the past — giving people free rein brings in outrageous concepts, but often some of them turn out to be do-able."

So much for getting an answer to my question. "Well," I said, "it'll make a change, anyway." I stood up to go.

Elizabeth stood, too. "You should know that I asked Marni and Carolyn to participate in the same exercise a few weeks ago, and they've already submitted their work." She leaned over the desk, shook my hand. "Thank you, Rosemary. Oh, and keep it quiet, will you? I don't want people spreading rumours."

I nodded — co-conspirator — but I had no clue what she was talking about. Rumours of what?

Chapter Thirteen

I worked harder on my Dream Book, as I called it, than I'd worked on anything since my days as a young keener.

In my idle mind time, I no longer refined my revenge fantasy, the one where I'm asked to become curator of the Costume Institute at the Metropolitan Museum of Art, inspire the creation of a high-end perfume (called *Rosemary* — can't you just smell it?), and have a torrid affair with Brad Pitt, all while Brian Turnbull's empire declines and falls and his new wife leaves him for a younger man.

Instead, I worked on story ideas for this imaginary *Panache*, the *Panache* of my dreams, as it were. Ideas came to me in exercise class, on the subway, while I plucked my eyebrows — even during my regular job, like at the combination fashion-beauty shoot I attended with Trish, the beauty editor.

There we were, Trish and I, in the photographer's studio, picking at a cheese tray while the model, a girl named Honey MacDonald, had her hair touched up for the sixteenth time.

"Hey, Trish," I said. I spread some Stilton on an apple wedge. "Don't you think that if the readers only knew how long it takes to get Honey to look good they'd feel less inadequate?"

Trish was still preoccupied by boyfriend problems. "Sorry?"

"Before I worked here, I might have looked at the finished photograph of Honey and thought all she had to do to make her hair flip over her head like that was to comb it that way. I might have believed she was wearing only blush on her cheeks, like you'll claim in the copy, instead of five pounds of concealer and foundation and powder. In other words, I might have thought the reason I don't look as good as her is because I'm an inferior being."

Trish shifted her chair away from me. "How long have you been at this job?"

"I'm just thinking . . . what if we ran a flawless finished photo of

Honey, then deconstructed the whole process next to it? We could start with her looking terrible when she got here at eight a.m., then do a countdown, take a picture of each stage. List two hours for makeup, one hour hair, a half-hour dressing her, a half-hour adjusting the lighting, shooting the Polaroids, blah blah blah, for a total of four hours to that carefree look. We could show the stylist taping up her tits, show the sweater being pinned and tucked at the back, even show Carolyn improving Honey's jawline on the computer back at the office.

"We could take one photograph each month, do the number on it, call it something like, 'Looks Perfect, But . . .' It'd be sort of neat, don't you think?"

"Wouldn't that be defeating our whole purpose, though? If the readers don't think the advertisers' products will make them look like the models, what's the point?"

"And I thought *I* was cynical."

Trish pushed herself up from the chair. "I need a coffee. And I think you need a Valium."

I sat there, mind steaming. Maybe this deconstructionist thing was bigger than one story idea. Maybe my whole Dream Book should hinge on it, should centre on this theme of the truth behind the façade. I could run a monthly feature on Celebrity Secrets, for instance. I could see readers wanting to know how many hair-grooming aids Jennifer Aniston uses on that coif of hers, or how many sit-ups Janet Jackson does every day before breakfast to maintain her rock-hard midriff.

Assuming we could get our hands on all this info, of course, but who cared about that right now, when this whole Dream Book thing was supposed to be an exercise in fantasy anyway?

In the middle of all this was Julie and Don's fifteenth wedding anniversary party, a big do at their house on a Saturday night.

"Do I have to come?" I'd asked when she'd called me two months before to set the date. "Shouldn't it just be your couple friends?"

"You'll be the sole family representative, with Mom and Dad still in Florida. Be there."

On party day, I slept in till nine, took a morning step class, and cooked myself a brunch of baked eggs with feta and mint, accompanied by whole grain toast and oven-roasted potatoes. The afternoon I spent working on my Dream Book. So I'll admit that by the time seven o'clock rolled around I was feeling a little restless, in need of some human company, though not necessarily of the Rosedale crowd.

I wrapped up an Indigo Girls CD in shiny silver paper, stuck blue stars all over the package, and attached the card I'd picked out, a photograph of a field of wooden chairs painted in different shades of blue, green, and violet.

To wear, I settled on a long black knit dress. Over it, I buckled a wide leather belt hung with miniature forks, knives, and spoons made out of silver. On my feet, my high-cut black Doc Martens. To further illustrate that my ordinary-person dressing phase was over, I plunked a hat on my head — a soft black velvet job, with a pocket watch face hanging from a crimson ribbon pinned to the brim. I did the makeup, checked my reflection, and saw my usual I'm-not-from-round-these-parts self. I picked up the black leather backpack I was calling a purse that season and considered for a second transferring the essentials into an evening bag, but I was already running late. I wrapped myself in a coat, hefted the backpack over my shoulder, and stepped out.

I let myself in the unlocked front door at Julie's and fought an urge to walk back out when I saw the guests clustered in Julie's centre hall, when I heard the party sounds. I smiled vaguely at people — Don't approach me, my smile said, I know what I'm doing — and headed upstairs. I threw my coat on Taylor's bed and reluctantly decided against drawing moustaches onto his Claudia Schiffer and Cindy Crawford pin-ups. On the way back down, I checked my reflection in a large mirror hung in the landing. I'd looked fine at home, but here I looked underdressed.

I plunged into the party and was engulfed by a bunch of the seventy-five people Julie had told me she was inviting. Some I recognized, some I didn't, but they almost all matched — the men in business suits, the woman in cocktail dresses and pearls.

I went looking for Julie in the front room and found Grahame. He was dressed up, in chinos and a button-down shirt, hair carefully combed to the side. He was carrying a tray of crostini.

"Hi, Grahame." I bent down and kissed him and almost flipped the food onto the floor in the process.

"Do you want one of these?" he said. His eyes were glued to the tray.

I picked up a piece of bread and bit into it — it was still warm, crunchy around the edges, and spread with chopped black olives and gorgonzola. Toothsome. "So, Grahame, feel like playing some Sega after? I could meet you in the family room in ten."

He shook his head, but only slightly, still watching that tray. "Maybe later. I have to serve these. I told Mommy I would."

I made my way over to a table set up by the window, where a bartender was dispensing drinks. I chose a flute of champagne, lifted a piece of sushi from a serving dish and kept moving, on the lookout for Julie, Don and some sign of dinner.

I found Don in a corner of the dining room, deep in conversation about golfing in New Brunswick. I patted him on the back as I passed. He waved, pointed to my hat, made a face like he thought it was crazy, and continued with his conversation. I waved back and pushed open the swinging door to the kitchen.

Julie was in there, talking to a chef in whites. Two helpers, trim young women in black trousers, bow ties, and white shirts, bustled about arranging food on platters. "Hi, Rosemary," Julie said, "I was wondering where you were. You look nice."

"So do you." She was in a clingy deep green velvet dress, ankle-length. With her tall, thin build, her long neck, her hair swept up into a chignon, she was stunning.

She started to say something else, but one of the waitpeople asked her a question. I moseyed off and sipped my champagne. The slight buzz it sent my head got me thinking how much easier this party would be to deal with if I got high. And, I recalled, I had a rolled joint tucked away in my bag. But where to smoke it? I walked through to the den at the back of the house and tried to remember if its windows opened. The door was ajar. I knocked, and Taylor's breaking voice spoke up. "The washroom's across the hall."

I walked in. "Hi, Taylor. Whatcha doing?"

He leaned back and stretched. "I'm *trying* to do homework." He was sitting at the computer, papers and books spread out beside him. Unlike his brother, he had not dressed for the party — his turtleneck, plaid flannel shirt, and jeans looked like he'd slept in them.

I pointed to the door. "You're not planning to get out there and mingle?"

"Have they served dinner yet?"

"My sentiments exactly." I bent down and looked at the screen. "What are you working on? History? English?"

"Environmental studies."

"Oh."

"And I have to get to it." He scrunched up his face. "Sorry, but."

"No, I get it." I thought of the joint again. "Maybe I'll go for a stroll in your backyard until dinner's ready."

He had already resumed keying, his eyes intent on the screen.

I walked to the back door and looked out the window at the immense lot Julie and Don called a garden. Outdoor lighting illuminated patches of the landscape — some bare branches of shrubs close by, the brick-paved path that meandered along between the now-empty flowerbeds, and down there by a stand of trees, the shadowy form of their garden bench.

I opened the door — it was already unlocked — felt a draft, and grabbed a tweed jacket hanging on a hook by the door. Don's, I guess. I threw it over my shoulders and slipped out.

The cool air in the dark night was bracing after the loud hot brightness of indoors. I walked over to the bench, sat down, pulled the joint out of my backpack, stuck it in my mouth, flicked on my lighter, and almost screamed when a voice said, out of nowhere, "Here for a smoke?"

In one quick movement, I eased off on the lighter and dropped it and the joint in my bag. I looked around in the dim light. "Who's there?"

A figure separated itself from a dark corner of the house and walked over. "Sorry, I didn't mean to scare you. It's Max Appelbaum. I'm doing the catering here tonight."

Relief. "Oh, hi. It's me, Rosemary. Julie's sister. You *did* scare me for a second. I thought I was alone out here."

"Mind if I sit down?"

I shook my head.

"Go ahead and smoke," he said.

Oh, what the hell. I pulled the joint back out, lit it with as much Lauren Bacall cool as I could muster, and held it out to him. "Want some?"

"What? No. Hey. Is that grass? It smells good." He did a double take. "Are you sure you're Julie's sister?"

I smiled. "Actually, I was adopted."

"Yeah," he said, "I used to feel that way about *my* sister sometimes, too." He drank from the beer bottle he held.

Through the smoke filtering into my brain, it occurred to me that he thought I'd been joking about being adopted, which was a novel reaction. I blew out smoke. "So if you're doing the catering, how come you're out here?"

"Julie invited me to the party, and I dropped in to make sure everything was going okay. But I had to get out of the kitchen — I make my staff too nervous." He placed his beer bottle on the ground. "You know, maybe I *will* have a toot, if you don't mind."

I passed over the joint and watched him take a toke. "You know how to inhale. Did you used to smoke?"

"Cigarettes? Yeah. You?"

"For fourteen years. Started when I was sixteen. Got up to two large packs a day."

He passed the joint back to me. "Come on."

"For real. I even have this incredibly clichéd picture of me in journalism school, sitting at a typewriter, lit cigarette hanging from my lips."

"So why'd you quit?"

"I started to feel nauseous every time I had a cigarette."

"That'd do it. Me, I stopped when my fingers turned yellow. I still dream about it, though. I wake up feeling guilty after a totally satisfying dream drag."

"I've had those dreams, too. It's some sort of psychological syndrome — your unconscious mind warning you off starting up again. We ran an item about it in the *Panache* health section one time."

"Really? Gee, maybe I should start reading *Panache*."

I stubbed out the roach on the ground. "Don't. It's mostly crap."

"Is that what they taught you at journalism school?"

I smiled. "Yeah, it is, actually. They were very into making the distinction between U and non-U journalism. What a joke."

"Ready for a career change, are you?"

I shrugged. "I guess. Unfortunately, there's not much demand out there for ex-fashion editors."

"You know what?" Max said, after a minute. "I think I may have gotten off. Do people still say that? To get off?"

"Sounds good to me. In a retro kind of a way."

There was another pause, but not an uncomfortable one.

"So how come *you're* not inside partying?" he said.

"Not my kind of crowd."

"Not trendy enough for you?"

"Nothing like that. I just don't fit in." I kicked out my feet.

"Must be your shoes." He stuck out a foot and placed his Doc Martens next to mine.

The toes of our shoes touched for a moment, then he swung his foot back under the bench.

I shivered. "Think the food's being served yet?"

"Soon. You like to eat?"

"Usually."

"So has Julie talked you into coming to Great Tastes?"

"I don't think so. What is it?"

"It's happening next week. Your basic huge food event to raise money for cancer research. A bunch of chefs set up stations for the night in a hotel ballroom and cook something fabulous, and everyone wanders around sampling."

"And you'll be cooking?"

"No, one of my chefs will be. I'm working behind the scenes. 'Food Co-ordinator' is my official title. Julie put me up to it. A friend of ours from law school's on the organizing committee."

"You were in law school with Julie?"

He stood and offered me a hand up. "Yeah. Don't I look like a lawyer?"

Of course he didn't look like a lawyer in his leather jacket, black jeans, the Doc Martens, that crazy short hair sticking up, his round gold-rimmed glasses.

We walked back up the path toward the house. "Julie never told me about knowing you from law school."

He opened the back door and stood aside for me to enter. "I'm sure you two have more exciting things to talk about."

I took off Don's jacket and hung it up on the hook.

"My glasses are fogged up," Max said. He squinted while he

wiped them off on his shirttail, then brought his face close to mine. "Are my eyes red?" he whispered.

I looked into his eyes — much bigger and browner when not diffused by his glasses — and giggled. "Yes."

He fixed his glasses on his face, pointed at my waist and smiled.

"What?" I turned toward him and heard the cutlery around my middle jingle.

"Great belt," he said.

Chapter Fourteen

My Dream Book was almost done.

I used the computer to lay out headlines and sample opening paragraphs for my proposed monthly columns. For something called, "Behind the Scenes at *Panache*: What we really do around here," I wrote a whole story, featuring day-in-the-life profiles of various key *Panache* staff. I threw in a little sophomoric humour and illustrated it with some Polaroids I'd taken around the office, including one of Carolyn sitting in the lap of a hunky young (gay) art assistant she'd hired, another of Trish glaring at me from behind a light table. *I* thought the piece was hilarious.

I'm no photographer, but I'd taken my camera along to a real shoot, too, to get some pix for that deconstructionist idea I'd had. And I'd cut out pictures from the contact sheet showing the model arriving with dark circles under her eyes and limp hair pulled back into a ponytail, followed by shots illustrating her step-by-step transformation into an air-brushed beauty.

But my favourite bit was the main fashion story I'd roughed out, called "Unrequited Love," which came about like this:

I was shuffling through some head sheets from a male model agency, one of those books containing stats on each guy, with four representative shots: sporty, intellectual, beefcake, sullen. This was for my real work, not my Dream Book — I was trying to find someone for a shoot we were doing on summer dresses that was supposed to be situated at an old-time carnival midway. The girl would be sweet and funky, in flowered tea dresses, clogs on her feet, her sexy innocence a contrast to the weathered carnies. The male model was supposed to be a carnie, too, if carnies ever looked like Jason Priestley. We wanted a guy who could carry off tight jeans, scuffed cowboy boots, a cowboy hat, and a snug-fitting T-shirt with the sleeves rolled up (a pack of Export As stuck inside the sleeve) to reveal power biceps. And he needed to have the kind of hair that looks good seriously greased back.

So I'm flipping through this book of male models trying to find the right look, skipping past the tough guys with the ultra-short hair and the stubble, and past the young sensitive types with earrings and long hair, and wishing we could just pay Jason Priestly some huge sum and be done with it, when one face leapt off the page. Not at all the face I was looking for, but it caught my eye.

He was in his mid-to-late twenties, I guessed, this guy. Good-looking in a boring way — the kind of fair, blue-eyed combination I would have drooled over in high school, but not the sculpted cheekbones and gelled pompadour look that was current, that I was seeking. Yet one shot on this guy's sheet stood out — the one in which he wore an Italian suit and band-collared shirt unbuttoned at the neck, cord-like tendons around his Adam's apple nicely exposed. I stopped my flipping and squinted, to blur the image, and saw Brian Turnbull in the face. Different colouring, different nose, but there was something in the eyes. And maybe the neck.

Suddenly, I had an idea for the Dream Book.

It was kind of immature if you knew where it was all coming from, but who would know? And I'd vary the details a little bit, make it distant enough from life that only I could recognize the players. Well, and Helen, too, probably, if she ever saw it, but she wouldn't, because the Dream Book was intended only for the eyes of Elizabeth Crowley. And Elizabeth hadn't been around when Brian and I had been an item, only at the tail end, that time in New York, when we hardly saw each other anyway, what with Marni acting ogre-ish.

So, how did it go, this idea?

We take our blond male model, and we put him in a suit He's a banker or a lawyer, dressed conservatively, not in Italian tailoring. More the WASPy American look, the Ralph Lauren type of image. Newport and all that, Connecticut.

I ask you, Is this similar to Brian? Hardly.

Okay. We style the hair so it's off the face but still has some movement. Then we sit him down in a meeting room with his sleeves rolled up, and — no, wait.

Start over. He's dressed the same, but the setting is an engagement party. See the elegant country home in the background. See the tables laid out on the huge back lawn under the spreading maple trees. See the white linen tablecloths, loaded with trays of tea sandwiches — cucumber and smoked salmon on thin brown bread with the crusts cut off. And throw a white iced cake in there, decorated with candied violets, no, real violets, tied with white satin ribbon. Think *Martha Stewart Living*. Got it. Lots of gleaming sterling silver, thick cloth napkins, gold-rimmed white china. Gross. But yes, that's it, that's what I want.

The fiancée stands at his side — she's blonde, too, and dressed in a pastel shade — pale mint maybe? Something to emphasize her virginal quality.

There she is, greeting guests, gesturing to her fine upstanding fiancé, who's not paying attention, who's looking in the wrong direction. Who's fascinated by the caterer, that exotic-looking Asian woman, no, make her black, or Indian, from India, yes, to avoid the personal connection but still get the point across, yes. The Indian woman is very accomplished, very cultured — you can tell from the blunt cut of her hair, from the simplicity of the sterling silver cuff on her wrist. And she's dressed in a chic sleeveless dress — Prada, let's say — which shows off her lean muscled arms.

Next page. Our hero is decked out in white flannels, cricket clothes almost, more Ralph Lauren, and *now* his sleeves can be rolled up to showcase his forearms, because it's a sunny spring day and he's at a posh horse field, set up with a yellow-and-white-striped tent, watching his fiancée jump horses.

No. Way too obvious. Try something else. Playing polo? Too close. Swimming? No, no swimsuits. Okay, keep on with the upper class theme, and try out, what? Croquet?

I've got it. Tennis. Move him to the stands at a tennis club, keep him in a white V-neck sweater with stripes around the V, and have him wear shorts this time, so we can see his blond hairy legs. He's watching his fiancée finish off her opponent in a singles match, or he's supposed to be watching, but instead, he's eyeing some gorgeous — fine, now we can say Asian woman. She's sitting at a poolside table under an umbrella, dressed in a linen suit, an open briefcase beside her, talking business on a cellular phone, CEO material for sure.

And so it goes, each page of ten, showing our hapless groom being drawn over and over to someone who looks more accomplished and chic and visibly part of a minority than his bland young wife will ever be. Take him through the tasteful bachelor dinner at a restaurant (check the black restaurant owner in a cocktail dress conferring with her staff in the background), on to the wedding (who's that spunky photographer wearing the Navajo choker?) and to the finale, where our poor hero realizes that what he wants more than the pink and white wife and the pink and white baby she produces is the competent and polished-looking Eurasian obstetrician who has just delivered their child.

Kind of petty this may all sound, but boy, was it fun. To plan, to conceptualize, to write up for Elizabeth. And to come up with the crap I wrote to support it: politospeak about showcasing both classic and trendy styles to appeal to the full spectrum of our readership, about the importance of presenting positive alternative images of beauty to counter the dominance of Caucasian role models in magazines today. With a reference to the changing demographics of the female fashion magazine consumer in the eighteen-to-forty-four age bracket, and to the concentration of fashion followers among twentysomething ethnic readers.

No mention of tweaking Brian in there, of course. My little private joke.

When the "Unrequited Love" write-up was finished, my Dream Book was complete. I handed it in to Elizabeth on deadline.

"I don't know how many of these ideas would really fly," I said, "but I had fun working on this project. Thanks for asking me."

She browsed through my pages and shot me a surprised look. "Well, I don't know when, but I'll be getting back to you on this. Very interesting. Thank you."

Chapter Fifteen

I climbed into Julie's car and into her floral scent. "Thanks for picking me up. Sorry I had to work late. Marni and Helen will be back from Europe tomorrow, thank god. Think there's any food left?"

She pulled out into the traffic. "It only started at seven — we haven't missed much. You look nice."

I didn't think so. It had been raining, and I'd been in and out all day, and my hair was in flat mode. To compensate, I'd applied extra mascara and lipstick, but I couldn't shake the bad-hair-day feeling. "Well, I'm hungry, anyway. I didn't really have time for lunch — I only had a few bites of some weird grain salad at a shoot. How about you? How was your day?"

"Good — everyone was on time for their various activities, including the babysitter. Plus I'm looking forward to this party, aren't you?"

"I was, until I found out Carolyn Whiting was coming. She has some new rich boyfriend who is — are you ready? A society dentist. Like, what is that, a society dentist? Apparently he goes to charity events like Great Tastes all the time. I can't wait to hobnob with that pair."

"There'll be so many people there you probably won't even see them."

"I can only hope."

We entered the enormous ballroom and stopped to admire the job done by the interior design team — the barnlike space had been transformed into a fantasyland of trees and flowers and skirted tables tied with garlands of ivy.

We walked around, checking out the fare at each chef's station. "Look," said Julie, "there's Max. We'll catch him later."

She pointed across the room where I could just make out the figure in a dark suit that must have been Max, talking to a gesticulating chef.

"Hey, cool," Julie said. "Quail eggs. What do you think? No?"

We walked past a long line-up for shrimp on skewers. "Did Max bring his mushroom-grower friend?" I said.

Julie looked blank.

"As his date, I mean."

"He doesn't have anyone to bring."

"But you said — "

"I'm definitely going to try that rice noodle thing there."

"Julie. I'm asking you something."

"What?"

"About Max. Is he involved with someone or not?"

"No. Why?"

"Just curious."

At the next cart, I smelled curry. "How old is he, anyway?"

"Did you see those tomatoes? Don't they look good for this time of year?"

"Julie!"

"How old is Max? He's thirty-eight. Unlike me, he fast-tracked to law school."

"And he never married."

"He lived with a woman for a long time. What was her name? Chantal? No. Louise? No. Anyway. She was a dancer."

I stopped walking. "Oh, great. There's Elizabeth Crowley."

Elizabeth stood near the next food station, garbed in a little black dress. Standing beside her with three cameras slung around his neck was Simon Wong, my favourite photographer.

Simon saw me, smiled and waved.

To Julie, I said, "Now that my whole office is here, I guess I should go over and say hello."

"Meet you at our table — number twelve. Bring food."

I sidled up to Simon, who was a goofy young guy with waist-length hair and rubber bracelets. "Having fun yet?" I said.

"What are you doing here, Rosemary? Somehow I didn't picture you for the fund-raising scene."

"I came with my sister. What's shaking?"

He motioned with his head to Elizabeth, who was standing talking to two locally famous stockbrokers. "We're cruising for celebrities."

"Find any yet?"

"No one too exciting."

Elizabeth finished up her conversation and came over. "Hello, Rosemary. I didn't expect to see you here. I'll get Simon to take our picture. But who with, I wonder?" She scanned the partygoers, looking for likely candidates.

"I know the guy who's co-ordinating the food."

"Perfect. Could you bring him over?"

I found Julie in a line-up for hand-formed nitrate-free beef sausage, told her not to get me a portion and that the photo shouldn't take long. Then I nabbed Max, who was consulting with a chef serving warm salmon sashimi with polenta timbales.

Max looked kind of cute in his navy suit, taupe shirt, tropical print tie. "Hi, Rosemary," he said. "Great you came."

I asked him if he'd mind having his picture taken, he agreed, and we headed back across the floor. "How's it going?" I said.

"It seemed like a good idea at the time."

"Come on, everything looks great."

"You mean it doesn't show that we've narrowly averted several disasters in the last hour alone?"

"Not at all. And I can't wait to start eating."

"Well, you didn't hear it from me, but stay away from the scallops."

When the photo-taking was done, Max shook hands with everyone and said he hoped to see me later, and I remembered that (a) I was starving and (b) Julie was still waiting for me at table twelve. I headed for the carts serving roasted corn, curried potatoes and peas, and seafood risotto. A good twenty minutes later, I carried my stack of small plates over to Julie and placed them on the table.

"Sorry," I said.

She pushed a glass of wine in my direction. "It's okay. I've been chatting with our tablemates. You looked important over there. People were staring. How'd it go?"

"Fine. I'll see if I can convince Helen to run something — she looks after *Panache*'s 'Out and About' section. But that's enough work for one evening." I picked up an ear of corn and took a big bite.

"Hello there, Rosemary," said Carolyn's voice behind me.

I turned around and faced the vision in a black lace slip dress that was Carolyn, her cleavage at my eye level. "Oh, hi, Carolyn," I said, with no enthusiasm.

We did the introductions, and I tried to cover my corn-filled teeth with my lips, which made for some weird elocution, but I was polite enough to wipe my buttery hands on a napkin before shaking with Carolyn's society dentist boyfriend, who had divorce, hair-transplant, and looking-for-a-younger-second-wife written all over him, but who otherwise seemed pleasant.

"I knew I'd find you eating," Carolyn said. Kind of a stupid thing to say, seeing as the whole point of this affair was to eat. Though knowing her, a woman who'd come out in her underwear when it was winter outside, she planned to have a salad and a glass of wine and call it a night. The dentist asked for directions to the curry and set off, but Carolyn sat down in an empty chair beside me, close enough that I could smell the wine on her breath.

"Not hungry?" I said to her. "I hear the scallops are good."

Julie stood up. "I need dessert. I'll be back."

Carolyn watched her go. "How long have you been here, Rosemary?"

"About an hour. You?"

"We came early and had a few drinks in the hotel bar. And I could have sworn . . . have you seen Elizabeth here tonight?"

"Yeah. She's wandering around with Simon Wong taking pictures."

"I must have been mistaken. Never mind."

I rooted around in my purse for a toothpick. "Okay, spill it, Carolyn. The suspense is killing me."

She leaned closer and rested her breasts on the table, which made them swell even higher than they were already pushed by her bra. I picked at my teeth and tried to keep my eyes from popping at the sight of all that flesh.

"You know Brian Turnbull?" she said.

Might as well have poured cold water on my head. My eyes lifted from her chest. "Yeah. What about him?"

"Well, Geoffrey and I were sitting in the bar having a glass of wine" — or two or three — "and I look up and see a man getting off the elevator, in a suit and overcoat, carrying a briefcase. I only saw him for an instant. But there was something about him that reminded me of Brian — that same swagger. You know what I mean?"

I noticed Max heading across the room in the direction of our table. I kept focused on Carolyn's face. "Go on."

"And I'm thinking, But what would he be doing in Toronto? And then, two minutes later, the elevator door opens again and there's Elizabeth, coming out in her overcoat and briefcase. But it couldn't be, right?"

Max was closing in. "What couldn't be?"

She leaned closer. "The two of them having an affair."

Was she drunk? Brian here? An affair with Elizabeth? Nothing about this story made sense.

"Am I interrupting?" Max said.

Carolyn switched to her charm-the-guys voice. "Not at all. Hi, there. Would you like to sit down? I was just leaving."

Max looked her in the eye, which I knew from recent experience was a difficult thing to do when there was so much else that was black or bare or edged in lace to look at. "Don't leave on my account."

"I wish I could stay and chat," she said, "but I should go find my honey. See you later, Rosemary." She rose and wiggled away.

Max sat in the seat she'd vacated and loosened his tie. "Who was that?"

"Some nutcase from my office."

"Hot body."

I felt that old familiar stab, that always-the-bridesmaid feeling, though I've actually done it only once, for Julie, when I was sixteen.

I poured him a glass of wine. "Here. Have you eaten?"

"Thanks. No, I haven't, and I probably won't. I get too close to the food." He drank some wine. "You know what this reminds me of, though, in a way? When I was in university, and I'd be up late studying, and I'd call four different Chinese restaurants. I'd order my favourite dish from each one, then go pick it all up on my bicycle. Did you ever do that?"

"No, but great concept. I know what I'd get, too — chicken with peanuts from Peter's Chung King, dim sum from Pearl, Cantonese chow mein from Sai Woo — "

"Not Sai Woo. Not that sixties-style food." He smiled, teasing. "I'd have thought someone like you would be more into the authentic cuisine."

I felt my hair coming to life, rising on my scalp like a jeopardized cat's. "What do you mean, someone like me?"

A puzzled expression crossed his face. "Someone who's into food."

Julie returned with a plate of tiramisu and two forks. "Hi, Max. You've done a wonderful job."

He leaned over and kissed her on the cheek. "What's good is having normal people to hang out with like you guys." He lowered his voice. "These high-flyers wear me out sometimes, even if some of them are my customers."

"This is nothing," I said. "You should try the fashion crowd in force, if you want to be worn out."

He touched my hand. "Is that a dare?"

My heartbeat knocked on my ribcage — flirt alert. *Don't be pathetic. You don't even like this guy.*

"Well," I said to Max, "next time I'm invited to something outrageously trendy, I'll be sure to think of you."

"I'll look forward to it," he said.

Chapter Sixteen

On the way to work the next day, I bought Helen a few stalks of freesia and a gingerbread woman, which I planned to leave on her desk as a welcome back surprise. But when I walked around her partition, there she was, at eight-twenty, unpacked and working.

"Hey — hi." I handed over the presents. "You're here early."

She grinned. "Still on European time."

I took the lid off my coffee cup and took a sip. "Was it fun?"

She smiled some more and giggled. "Yeah."

I was actually in a better mood than I'd been for a while, but I was finding her cheeriness a little grating. "So when do I hear the stories?"

"You ready now? I've got tons. Let's go into your office."

At my desk, she dished the dirt, gave me all the gossip, told me about Robert Altman filming a movie in Paris at the collections, about seeing Sophia Loren and Kim Basinger and everybody up close.

"So what about Marni?" I said. "How'd that go?"

"I didn't see much of her. She palled around with some TV people mostly, kept disappearing for hours on end. Not that I cared." The silly grin danced over her face again.

"Okay, I'll bite. Why didn't you care?"

"Because I met this guy."

"Start at the beginning."

His name was Sean Latimer, from Montreal. Twenty-eight, an MBA, had worked in a bank for several years, recently took over his father's leather goods business. They met in the line-up at Gaultier.

"Come on," I said, "I want more details. Did you dance? Did he buy you dinner? Is he single? Give."

Helen's face crumpled up. "I think I'm in love."

And my heart quavered in response. Because I was happy for her, and because I couldn't imagine having that look on my own face. "So when are you going to see him next?"

"In ten days. He comes to Toronto on business all the time. And when I got in last night, there was a message on my machine saying he missed me, and he sent flowers to my apartment, and I can't wait till next Friday."

I remembered that feeling. "Well, that's certainly the best story of the lot."

"I think you're right," she said, all dreamy. *Enough now.* I pitched my coffee cup into the waste basket. "Well, it's great to have you back. It was getting kind of lonely around here."

"Thanks," she said, but I could see as she floated out that her mind was elsewhere, and would be for a while.

After Helen had gone, I logged onto my E-mail and found a message from Elizabeth asking me to come see her. At the appointed hour I beamed myself up, walked in, and saw she held my Dream Book in her hands.

"I was really impressed with this," she said, by way of greeting. "*Really* impressed." She turned her X-ray vision on me, trying to detect a secret identity behind my dull exterior, I guess.

"Gee, thanks. I had fun doing it." I'd told her that before, I know, but you've got to say things twice to these senior-exec types — they don't remember much from one day to the next, let alone from one week to another. It's supposed to be a status thing — like important people only remember important things.

Elizabeth turned the pages of my book. "Of course, some of these ideas are over the top, but . . ." She stopped at what looked, upside-down, like the Unrequited Love story, and low-grade tremors rumbled through my insides. "This story in particular, I liked. Very original. And the justification you wrote based on reader demographics really spoke to me. It was more strategic than the usual rationale I get from the editorial group."

"Full of surprises, that's me."

She shut the book. "I'd like you to produce this story."

Earthquake time. "You're joking, right?"

"I said I really liked the idea, and your write-up shows your enthusiasm for it. So — do it. With modifications, of course, to allow for a reasonable budget."

Something told me I was supposed to stand up. I stood up. "I'll mention it to Marni, then, shall I? Or will you?"

"Mmm. Yes. Marni. Why don't you tell her? If she has any questions, she can speak to me. Thank you, Rosemary." She looked at her calendar. "You should be able to make the June issue, right?"

I looked at the calendar, too, though I knew June was completely planned. "That might be tight, unless we bump something."

"See what you can do. Oh, and I asked Simon Wong to send the proofs from last night's party to you today. Also for June. Can you pass them on to whoever? Thank you."

I went downstairs, made a couple of copies of the Unrequited Love proposal, and decided to see Marni right away, get it over with.

I found her alone in her office.

"Hi, Marni. How was your trip?"

She spoke in an unnaturally deep voice. "Fine," she said, only she stretched the word out extra long, like, "Fiiiiine." God, she was weird.

"Good," I said. "Listen, while you were away, Elizabeth asked me to put together some new ideas for that brainstorming project. Same as you and Carolyn."

She paled under her powder and spoke in her normal voice. "I'd love to see your ideas, Rosemary."

"Sorry, I handed them all in."

"Didn't you keep a copy?"

"Only of some parts. Other parts had this unusual format that was just too . . . Anyway, believe it or not, Elizabeth told me she wanted us to produce this one really crazy story idea I had. So, here it is" — I handed her the proposal — "for June, Elizabeth was thinking."

Marni started to read. "Call me," I said, and dashed out.

But I'd not gone ten steps when I realized I'd left my pen on her desk. I charged back into her office to get it and found her gazing out the window, my proposal in her hands.

"My pen," I said. "I left it here." I reached for it, held it up to show her.

I expected her to give me an irritated stare, but the eyes she turned toward me looked more sad than angry. "Fine," she said, and bent her head to read my pages.

An envelope from Simon Wong marked RUSH was sitting on my desk. I picked it up, walked over to Helen's cubicle, and opened it. "These are for you," I said to Helen. "From this food fund-raising thing I went to last night."

She looked at the first sheet with a magnifying lens. "Good party?"

"It was okay. Not too relaxing, though, with Elizabeth there, not to mention Carolyn, tipsy, in black lace."

"Hey, who's this guy in the picture with you? He's kind of cute." She handed me the contact sheet and the loupe and pointed to a shot of Elizabeth, Max, and me.

"You think he's cute? He's short. He's a friend of my sister's. He organized the food." I handed back the sheet.

"Is he single?"

"Yeah. Why? Already your eye is wandering?"

"Not for me. For you."

I picked up a rubber band ball Helen had on her desk and tossed it up in the air. "He sort of asked me out, actually."

"So go for it."

"I don't know. I think he wears a smaller size in jeans than I do."

"Come on. He cooks, right? Think how good he must be with his hands." She did Groucho Marx with the eyebrows.

"Helen. Please. I came in here because I wanted to ask you something. While you were away, Elizabeth asked me to put together some pie-in-the-sky ideas, and this was one of them, and she wants us to do it for real, and I wanted to know what you thought." I handed her the proposal.

"You want me to read this now?"

Yes, I wanted her to read it now. All the way from Elizabeth's office and into Marni's I'd been reassuring myself that I'd changed the details of the stupid idea enough from the true Brian and Rosemary story that no one would recognize it. Helen was the test to see if I was about to make a total fool of myself. I tossed the rubber ball up and waited. Damn if she wasn't a slow reader. A bright person, but a slow reader.

She laughed when she came to the demographic stuff. "Where'd you get this crap?"

"You know how I love reading those market research reports."

She handed me back the paper. "I think it sounds kind of cool. Expensive. But different. How'd you come up with the idea?"

I checked her face. She wasn't being sarcastic. She hadn't seen through it.

"Where'd I get the idea?" I said. "Who knows? Maybe I dreamt it."

Chapter Seventeen

Typical Sunday afternoon: me lying on the couch in sweats reading the newspaper, TV on in the background, a bowl of grapes and a block of Jersey Nut on the coffee table.

The telephone rang. "Hi," said Julie. "You decent?"

"Oh, dressed to the nines, as usual, for a quiet afternoon at home. Why?"

"I wanted to stop over and drop something off in about half an hour. Okay?"

"Drop what off?"

"It's a surprise. Look nice."

I hung up, yawned, and went to look in my bathroom mirror, see how I was doing. Pretty scary is how. I washed my face, pencilled in some eyeliner, and decided the hair was too far gone for an easy fixing — I pushed it up on top of my head and stuck a barrette in any which way.

I wandered out into my living room to check its status — the only mess was the Sunday *New York Times* spread around. I picked up the sections, threw them into the recycling box. The rest of the room looked fairly neat, which was more due to the apartment's extreme lack of decoration than to my housekeeping habits. When the only furniture in a room is a couch, a coffee table, and a TV on a stand, it's not that difficult to keep tidy.

I sank down on the couch. I'd meant to do more of an interior design thing when I'd taken this place two years before, but I'd never gotten around to it. In an initial burst of energy, I'd picked out some bright colours and had the walls painted before I'd moved in — orange sherbet in the living room, lemon in the kitchen, mint in my bedroom, raspberry in the bathroom, white trim all round. I'd intended to acquire all manner of wonderful lamps, art, and furniture to highlight this colour scheme, but I hadn't. And now it was probably time to get the place repainted already.

Maybe there was some good decorating program on TV. I flicked it on and wasted half an hour sitting zombielike in front of a cooking show featuring an unappetizing low-fat vegetable soup, and was roused by the ring of my doorbell. I jumped up, turned off the TV, and answered the door.

Julie stood on the step, and the Fab Food van was parked in front of the house, with the rear doors open and what appeared to be Max's legs showing below. "Hi," Julie said. And whispered, "Fix your hair!"

I stepped out onto the porch in my stocking feet, my arms wrapped around me against the cold. "You've brought me a banquet?"

"Even better." Julie went back down the steps, joined Max at the rear of the van, and started tugging on something.

I went inside and slipped on shoes. When I came back out, Max and Julie had just pulled a dresser out of the van and set it down on the road. I walked over. "Hi, Max." I examined the dresser up close. "Wow, is this fabulous, or what?"

The dresser was wood, old-looking, had square edges. It stood about waist-high and had three wide drawers with round knobs on them. Unpainted, it wouldn't have been much to look at — something you'd reject at a flea market as without character. But now the frame was done in multiple shades of yellow: pale yellow and ochre and a fireballish tone all faded into each other. And each drawer was painted a different set of colours. The top one, in aqua and turquoise and sea greens, took me back to the waters of Biscayne Bay. The middle drawer was done in a bunch of related reds and magentas, like when they smear lipsticks all over the beauty pages in *Panache*. The third drawer was powder blue to royal to midnight blue, and it sparkled in one corner with tiny silver stars.

"Julie," I said, "this is so great. I love it."

Julie squeezed my arm. "You like it? Really?"

"Really. A lot. But why is it here?"

Julie and Max each lifted an end. I scurried around to support the middle and we all took baby steps up my front walk. Julie said, "I was hoping you'd keep it for me for a while. There isn't really any room in my basement, not if I plan to start on something else soon. And you have space, I figured. You don't mind, do you?"

"Mind? I want to own it. Wait. Put it down. I'll get the door."

They squeezed by me and placed the dresser on the floor in my living room. Max straightened up and took off his jacket, revealing a faded black T-shirt and biceps more defined than I would have expected. "Where do you want it?" he said.

I pulled my barrette out, ran my fingers through my hair, and pointed to one of the room's empty corners. When the dresser was in place, we stood back and watched it glow against my orange walls. "What do you think, Max?" I said.

"I think it's great. And I told Julie she should start looking for places to sell her stuff."

"He's right, Julie. You should."

"I'd need more than one piece before approaching anyone, and at the rate I'm going assembling a portfolio should take me about another ten years." She brushed something off the top of the dresser. "But thanks, guys, I'm glad you like it. We should go, Max." To me, she said, "He has to get the van back — someone's having a party tonight."

I picked up my backpack from the floor and pulled out my datebook. "Hey, speaking of parties, I've been invited to a press preview of the Craft Council show on the . . . the twenty-second. Why don't we go, Julie? Check out the competition."

Julie glared at me and tipped her head toward Max.

"All of us," I said to him. "Want to?"

Max zipped up his jacket. "But will the fashion crowd be there? That's what I want to know."

"Out in force, probably."

Julie hit her forehead with the heel of her hand. "Oh, no. I can't go. The twenty-second, you said? That's the first night of Taylor's hockey tournament, and I'm assistant coach. You two will have to go without me." She headed for the door.

Nice work, Julie.

Max hung back. "I should really check my schedule, too . . . I might have something else on."

I couldn't believe it. He was giving me an out. "Well," I said, "I sure hope you can make it."

Why not? Go out with the guy, get it over with, prove there was no chemistry between us.

"I hope so, too," Max said.

A few days later, Julie called me. "So, Rosemary, not to bug you constantly, but Grahame has talked me into organizing a family baseball game."

"Weren't you just saying something about hockey? How can it be time for baseball already?"

"I was thinking of this coming Friday. Five o'clock. At Rosedale Park. Adults and kids, a friendly few innings, back to our place afterward for a barbecue."

"A barbecue? In this weather?"

"And Grahame wants you to play."

"Ha ha."

"No, really. He read a children's book about a extended family ball game — all these cousins and aunts and uncles playing together — and now he's dead set on trying it out."

A pause while I thought about how much I don't like team sports, or, in fact, any game involving a ball.

"Rosemary? Come on. You can play outfield."

"Gee, thanks."

"You don't want him to think his only relatives are the ones on Don's side of the family, do you?"

"Oh, all right. I'll play. But I should warn you — we're shooting this week, and the last set-up is scheduled for Friday morning. It shouldn't go past noon, but I'm just saying."

"Better start warming up your arm."

"Maybe it'll snow."

But it didn't snow. In fact, that particular Friday dawned sunny and mild, and by the time I headed downtown at noon it was balmy: office workers were sitting out on building steps in their shirtsleeves, faces turned toward the sun, greasy hot dogs clutched in their hands.

I was doomed to play ball.

I hadn't made it in to the office until noon because I'd spent the morning at my apartment, presiding over the tail-end of that shoot I'd mentioned to Julie, which just happened to be the Unrequited Love shoot.

And why was the shoot happening at my place? Let's just say drastic changes had been made to the original concept to make it fit into our budget.

Luckily, the male model who'd originally caught my eye — his name was Peter Brunello, by the way — came cheap. And for the fiancée character, we'd gone with an unknown blonde girl, also inexpensive. But we'd really had to scramble on our locations. For the birth scene, we'd talked a brand-new nursing home into letting us use one of their medical rooms in exchange for some PR mentions. We'd posed the wedding party on some church steps for free. A restaurant which Elizabeth frequented agreed to play host to our bachelor dinner, and a public park tennis court subbed for the private club where our hero watched his fiancée while exposing his hairy blond legs. Though we had to shoot it pretty tight to hide the facts that no trees were in leaf, little bits of slush lay on the surface of the tennis court, and the legs in question were covered in goose-bumps.

But the set-up the budget just could not afford was the engagement party I'd imagined as the opening of the Unrequited Love story — the garden party at the country mansion. So the engagement party became a bridal shower at someone's apartment. My apartment. The scenario I'd come up with involved my front porch and Max's van. The bridal shower is over, and the maid-of-honour type stands on the porch, framed by some of that nice red Victorian brick around my front door. The hostess is waving goodbye to the bride, our hero carries out the loot in a bunch of shopping bags, and the aglow fiancée prattles to her beau about the shower, only he's distracted, not listening, too busy checking out the dark-skinned caterer directing her staff to load up the van.

That was the set-up we'd substituted, and that's what I'd been doing that Friday morning.

When I parked my car at Rosedale Park, I saw that people were already positioned around the main diamond. Throwing and catching were going on, but it seemed to be warm-up time still.

I walked over to the batting cage and watched Taylor slug a ball out to centre field, where Julie did a dramatic diving catch.

Grahame came over to me, holding a glove. "Hi, Rosemary. Want to use Dad's mitt?"

I took the soft weathered thing from him and slid my hand inside. "Thanks. Where's Don?"

"At the hospital. And Rosemary, Mommy told me you didn't know all the rules."

I crouched down to his eye level. "She's right. Tell me what I need to know."

"Well, you know which base is which, right? And about three strikes, you're out?"

"Yeah. Is that basically it?"

"No, there's another important rule: if you're on base, and the batter hits a pop fly, you can't run. Unless you tag up."

"You're losing me already."

He sighed. "Okay. Say you're on first. And I hit the ball out to centre field, and you start to run, but before you get to second base, Mommy catches the ball."

She probably would, too. "Got you so far."

"Well, you can't take a base on a pop-out, so you have to go back to first before Mommy throws the ball to first. Or if you're really fast, you could go back and touch first — that's called tagging up — and then run to second. Okay?"

I could tell he wouldn't want to explain it again, so I pretended I understood. I straightened up and shaded my eyes against the blaze of the afternoon sun. "Shouldn't we start the game soon?"

"I'll go get Max. He's the other captain." Grahame ran over to second base and spoke to a man who stood there whipping balls around in mean form but who was so backlit by the sun that I couldn't see his face. Though he had to be, of course, Max Appelbaum.

That Julie. At it again.

It wasn't that I didn't like Max. On the contrary, every time we'd met, I'd found him to be pleasant, amiable, easy to talk to. Hell, he even had a job. And he liked to eat — a character trait I value highly in people.

But something was missing. And I wasn't comparing him only to Brian either, to someone who sent me mind-blowing pheromone signals across the room the moment I first laid eyes on the guy. Well, maybe I *was* comparing him to Brian. Maybe Max's chest did seem like it would look scrawny compared to Brian's impressive pecs. Maybe Max's black jeans were sort of plain next to Brian's $2000 suits. And his laid-back manner a little soporific next to Brian's Type-A empire-building intensity. But even if Brian represented the most extreme edition of every crush I've ever had, that doesn't change the fact that with Max there was no tension, no pull. When I was around him, my breath didn't get caught in my throat, my skin didn't break out in hives, and every fibre of my being did not yearn for his touch.

So that when I reached third base on someone's pop, and everyone started yelling at me to run back, and I remembered a little late that this set of circumstances might have something to do with Grahame's rule, and I sprinted back to second, where Max stood, his arm out to catch the ball, and I somehow tripped him, and we both fell, and we ended up lying on the gravel, arms around each other — I did not feel anything. Aside from a bruised sensation on my leg where I'd fallen, and a general impression of soft curly hairs on his arm, and a hard body, and that he was actually taller than me, by maybe an inch, two at the most.

We untangled ourselves, and I helped him up, and we both said, "You okay?" and "I think so," and tried to ignore Taylor on first base, who had dropped his mitt on the ground so he could cross his index fingers and chant, "Max and Rosemary, sitting in a tree, K-I-S-S-I-N-G," etc.

Julie hovered over us. "Nothing broken?"

We brushed ourselves off and said No. She smiled. "You're out, by the way." She strolled back to the pitcher's mound.

I limped off the field and sat beside Grahame on the bench. "That was the rule I was telling you about," he said.

"And I'll never forget it again, I promise you."

He snapped and unsnapped his batting glove. "It's okay. I thought you'd strike out anyway. It was lucky you got as far as second."

"Gee, thanks. Listen, Grahame, I think I might sit out the rest of the game." I touched my leg. "Injury."

"You want a Band-Aid?"

I smiled and said No and watched him go warm up on deck.

The next time the sides changed, I stayed on the bench and took over the scorekeeping. Max came and sat next to me. "You recovered from the big spill?"

"Yeah. But let's face it: sports are not my thing."

"No?" He nodded at Julie, taking a lead-off at first in the kind of slim-fit jeans that can only be worn by people with thin thighs. "Doesn't it run in your family?"

"Well, no. Not exactly."

He turned and squinted at the sun hanging over the bare tops of the trees at the far end of the park. "I'd better get going. I'm supposed to be at a Sabbath dinner tonight."

I hadn't thought he was religious. "Your parents?"

"No, my aunt. My parents aren't observant. But my aunt does the Friday night dinner every week. And she occasionally invites me along so she can badger me about not being married when there are so many nice single Jewish girls around."

He poked at a hole in the finger of his baseball glove, where a leather strip hung, untied. "Well," he said, "until the next time we roll around on the ground."

I crossed out his name on the batting line-up and watched him walk away.

Chapter Eighteen

I stood in the middle of the halogen-lit, white-walled exhibition space, Helen at my side.

"Can we go eat now?" Helen said.

"Come on. Wasn't it nice to look at something other than clothes for a change?"

"I think I need a bigger change than going to a craft show."

"Can you see Max and Sean?"

"There's Max," she said, "in front of the green quilt." She waved him over. "And Sean went to the washroom. Should be back in a minute."

I looked at Helen. There were signs of tension around her eyes and mouth, a state that could have been partly due to the fact that she was wearing black over-the-knee stockings with high-heeled Mary Janes and a short A-line skirt — an ensemble she had the legs for, definitely, but that would make anyone wearing it tense, I would have thought.

"So what do you think of Sean?" she asked.

"He seems nice." We'd barely spoken, but my first impression had been of a toothy smile and charm of a type — he'd kissed me on both cheeks, on introduction, in that Montrealish way. Not a custom I happen to be fond of, but some people like that in a person. "How's it going with him?"

"Okay." She pulled up a stocking. "Though it's a bit awkward tonight. It takes a while to get used to each other again after we've been apart. You know?"

"Yeah." I thought of Brian, lifted my glass to take another sip of wine, and decided against it. I'd been feeling a bit off since coming home from work.

"I'm starving," Helen said. "I'm going to go find Sean. Meet you at the front door."

Max walked over. "Well," he said, "I may be biased, but I think Julie's dresser could hold its own here, don't you?"

I wiped my clammy palms on my cocktail napkin. Was it me, or was it hot in the room? "I bet it's hard to break into the scene, though."

"She'll find her way. You'll see."

Max and I headed for the door. "So how'd you like the crowd?" I asked him.

"Some of these people seem to think they're rather fabulous."

"Oh, but they are."

"No, *you* are," he said, "only you don't act it."

My stomach lurched. Okay, I'd have no more wine and go easy on dinner. I didn't want whatever bug I'd caught ruining an otherwise harmless evening.

In the car, Max said, "So, where to, folks?"

Helen looked at Sean. "How about Chinese food?"

"Sure," he said, "if you guys want."

"We could go to Pearl," Helen said.

Max: "Or Excellent Peking House."

Me: "Anyone for Lee Garden?"

Sean said, "What does it matter where we go? Chinese food is Chinese food."

A short silence from us three, then Max again: "Mandarin Paradise isn't far. Is that okay with everyone?"

Helen and I both said Yes right away, and I was grateful Max had come along.

The restaurant was full when we walked in, but there was no line-up. "Share a table?" a waiter asked. Helen and I looked at each other and both said No. The waiter pointed to a group of people who were paying their bill. "Wait one minute," he said and ran off to clear and wipe the plastic tablecloth.

Sean rubbed his hands. "You know what they say: if the Chinese eat here, it must be a good restaurant."

We sat down and opened our menus. I picked up the piece of paper and pen the waiter had left behind. "I vote for shrimp with eggplant."

Helen: "Definitely. And some noodles. Singapore okay?"

Max: "Sounds good. What about steamed pickerel?"

"Sure," I said.

Sean spoke up from behind his menu. "I'll have the chicken with cashews."

Helen said, "I think we're going to order a bunch of things and share." Like, duh.

"Well then, can we share the chicken with cashews?"

I started writing. "No problem. Chicken with cashews, number forty-six. There it is, written down. See? Now what else?"

Sean picked up a chopstick in each hand and started drumming on the table. "What are those things written in Chinese on the wall?" He pointed to some red paper strips covered with Chinese characters. "Those are probably the best dishes. What do those signs say, Rosemary?"

"I don't know, Sean. I can't read Chinese."

Sean turned to Helen. "What do they say?"

Helen began quietly explaining to him that she'd failed the written part of her Chinese language lessons when she was a kid. Max raised his menu and muttered from behind it, "What's with this guy? Why would he think you read Chinese?"

I raised my menu. "He probably thinks we all look alike, too."

Max's brow creased. "What?"

"You know. All Asian people."

He put down the menu. "I don't get it."

"What part don't you get?"

"You're not Asian."

"Sure I am — half."

"Come on."

"What? I'm telling the truth."

"And Julie? I suppose she's half-Asian, too?"

Sean and Helen were listening now. "No. Just me. I was adopted. She wasn't."

Max stared at me. "You're kidding."

"I'm not. Helen, is this true?"

Helen, wide-eyed, nodded.

Sean resumed drumming and said to Max, "You didn't know she was Oriental? I spotted it right away. It's all in the eyelids."

Max laughed.

My face was getting hot. "What's funny?"

"I'm sorry," Max said. "I'm not laughing at you. It's just that I told my aunt to stop with the matchmaking because I'm too attracted to a certain WASP shiksa." He leaned over and kissed me on the cheek, which action cranked up the jack-in-the-box in my stomach again.

"Look," I said, "let's just order."

After the waiter had whisked away the menus, Sean said to Helen, "You know, I think this is the first time we've had Chinese food together. Do you hold your bowl like this?"

He had to demonstrate, too, holding his empty soup bowl up near his face and miming a scooping movement with his chopsticks.

Obviously, Sean didn't know what I knew — how Helen felt about this topic. Obviously, Helen had not yet confided in Sean what she'd told me once when we'd gotten into a discussion about embarrassing things that parents do. When I'd cited my father's drinking habits and my mother's housedresses, and she'd complained about the way her parents ate.

Helen's face turned red, and she said No, she didn't lift her bowl. "Not when I'm with white people, anyway."

Major tense silence now, during which the waiter brought soup, or rather plunked down a large bowl on the table, said, "House soup," and departed.

And it looked awful, the soup — a brownish broth in which swam indeterminate pieces of gelatinous meat clinging to chopped-up bones. A mixture of appeal to some, I'm sure, but not, I could tell, my cup of tea.

"What is *that*?" said Sean.

Max ladled out bowls for each of us. "I believe the waiter called it house soup."

Helen picked up her soup spoon and started eating. And in the wake of her white people comment — though, at this point, I wasn't sure which camp she'd slotted me into — how could I do else but pick up my own spoon and express solidarity by partaking of the brackish liquid? I only hoped my stomach could stand it.

"Sorry about the double date from hell," I said to Max in the car, after we'd dropped off Helen and Sean. "But what am I going to tell Helen when she asks me tomorrow what I think? Or when she says, 'You think he's an asshole, right?' "

Max stared out the windshield. "I can't believe I didn't realize you were adopted before now. When I think back on some of the things I said . . . you must have thought I was a total idiot."

"No, not at all. Actually, it makes for a nice change to meet someone who's colour-blind."

"I guess it was partly the context — you were introduced to me as Julie's sister, and I accepted that. But I even saw a resemblance between you two — I still do. The way you walk, the way you roll your eyes, the shape of your earlobes."

The shape of my earlobes? Jumpiness again inside me, a mid-extreme case. I knew I shouldn't have eaten that soup. We pulled up near my house and he cut the motor.

"Listen," I said, "I'd ask you in, but I've been feeling a bit strange all day, healthwise. So, thanks a lot, sorry, and goodnight."

I had the door halfway open, so eager was I to sprint out and avoid the whole to-kiss-or-not-to-kiss issue. Especially with Chinese-food breath. Though we'd been given mints on the way out of the restaurant — those little pink and green and white pillow-shaped ones — and I'd grabbed a handful and chewed them down.

He unlatched his seatbelt. "I'll walk you to your door."

He linked arms to walk with me, in a friendly way, not aggressive or masterful like some would be, and in the late-night chill I didn't mind the warmth of his body beside mine.

"I had fun tonight," I said. "Despite Sean and feeling a bit queasy."

"You feel queasy?"

I nodded.

"Shortness of breath?"

Another nod.

"Stomach upset?"

"A little, why?"

"And rapid heartbeat?"

Oh no. Not a frustrated doctor.

He let his hand drop down to hold mine and said, "I've felt like that all day too. Because I was seeing you tonight."

What? No. No way. He wasn't trying to suggest I'd been feeling upside-down because of him — and then his arms were around me, and he was kissing me. Long, and slow, and with great sincerity. And I kissed back, grateful for having eaten the mints, breathing in his heady scent, and noticing that the kiss was a bit too wet and a bit too slobbery, but goddamn if it wasn't churning up the blood in the old sex organs anyway.

Chapter Nineteen

So no, he didn't stay over that night. Wouldn't even come in, though just as well, seeing as it was more libido talking than common sense when I invited him. On only our first date! What a slut. But anyway.

I went inside alone and turned on the lights and paced the room and felt all hot and cold. And stunned. Who would have believed that Max had quickened my pulse after all?

Worse, now that I'd finally deciphered the message my body had been sending me, there wasn't anything I could do about it. Because he was going away for a whole week, to New York, to a gourmet food trade show. "They're not much fun, these shows," he'd said when he stood on my front porch, hugging me in a way that didn't just make me hot for his body but warm and drowsy, too, like I could fall asleep right there, standing in his arms.

"Well, eat something good for me," I'd said, and gone inside to do some massive dream-building.

A few days after Max had gone, I was sitting in my office daydreaming about him, not even pretending to work, when Elizabeth Crowley called. Wanted me to come up right away and bring the proofs from the Unrequited Love shoot with me.

When I got to her office, she was sitting on the visitor side of the desk doing one of those we're-all-equals-except-I'm-the-boss poses. I ignored her gesture that I sit next to her and walked around the desk to sit in her high-backed executive chair.

She took it well. "I asked you up here," she said, "because *Panache* has been presented with a golden opportunity to build our franchise."

I nodded as if I knew what this meant, though I didn't, other than to be fairly sure she wasn't talking about opening up a donut shop.

"The National Opera Company is holding a gala fund-raising ball in June," she said. "They're organizing an evening wear fashion show as part of the entertainment, but I dined last night with the committee chairwoman and convinced her to add something a little more dramatic — more theatrical — to their show. A finale that will really create a buzz." She reached out a hand. "Did you bring the proofs?"

"Oh. Yeah. Here."

Elizabeth opened the file folder and looked at the pictures. "Oh, yes. These are good. This story's going to be fabulous on the runway."

"Am I hearing things, or are you talking about putting Unrequited Love on stage as the finale of this opera show?"

"Isn't it a great idea?" She kept looking at the proofs.

I set the mind in motion. Could it be done?

For the first segment, we could, I suppose, send our model, Peter the Brian-double, in a suit and tie — only pray he'd done runway before — out for a stroll, his pretty blonde fiancée on his arm. There, at the end of the runway, he stops, kneels down, and mimes proposing. Not bad. And she could make great hay out of accepting. Though it would help if he could slip a diamond ring on her finger — maybe we could talk some local jeweller into lending us a few significant rocks? Because that would be kind of cool, for her to extend her arm with a flourish, fingers angled up just so. Except that the brainless girl we'd used for the shoot would not do. I'd have to find someone else, someone who could really ham it up, play to the audience. Someone like — of course — MouMou.

Yeah, I could see her up there, also in a suit, but a sucky, not-for-work suit, a ladies-who-lunch suit. Yes, there she is, accepting a ring with overdone delight, and now the two of them are kissing, and he's turning in mid-kiss to eye a Chinese model striding by in Lacroix.

Not bad. But it would take some time to set up. "What's the date of this gala night?"

"May twenty-sixth. At the Grand Chateau." She pointed to one of the pictures on the contact sheet. "We could finish with this wedding scene. The traditional fashion show closing, but with a twist." She shut the file. "Okay, Rosemary?"

"Okay what?"

"Do it. Co-ordinate the project." She handed me a piece of paper. "Here are the names and numbers of the contact people at the opera. Get on it right away."

"Don't get mad, but why are we doing this again?"

She walked me to her door. "Think of the exposure. The high profile for *Panache*. The tie-in with the Unrequited Love story in the June issue. This kind of publicity is just what we need right now."

Whatever you say, boss.

The telephone rang on the Thursday, at about nine at night, when I sat at home, dance music blaring on the stereo, head bent over the wardrobe sequencing of Unrequited Love for the gala.

"Hi, Rosemary, it's Max."

The head-to-toe rippling of my internal fluids that I would come to recognize as the Max wave coursed through me. "Oh, hi. Where are you?"

"New York. I've been thinking about you, a lot. And I wanted to hear your voice."

Gulp. "How's your trip going?"

"Hectic. I've tasted enough new products to fill the whole store. But I found some good stuff and placed a few orders. How're you doing?"

"Good. Fine. I've been thinking about you, too." A silence fell, nervous-making. "So. See any shows?"

"Don't laugh. *Beauty and the Beast*. I got house seats from a friend."

"And?"

"It was a bit overcooked. My friend was fine, though. She played an eggbeater, among other things."

Oh, a female friend. A Broadway chorus girl friend. Hadn't Julie mentioned something once about Max living with a dancer? Tell me this wasn't going to be a So-I-looked-up-the-old-flame-and-the-next-thing-I-knew story.

"Rosemary? You still there?"

"Yeah. Sorry. I got distracted. I've been working on this big project for work — putting on a fashion show segment for an opera company benefit. All very glamourous and exciting and time-consuming as hell."

"That sounds good. Is it good?"

I looked up at the cobwebs on the ceiling of my living room and tried to make my voice sound like all I cared about was my career. "Yeah, it's great."

Another uncomfortable pause. "Well, if you're that busy, maybe this isn't the best time to ask you to dinner. That's why I called. For Saturday night, when I'm back. Or will you have to work?"

I stood up and kicked myself in the butt. "Saturday? Let me think. No, that should be okay. Even if I end up working during the day, I should be able to manage an evening off. Sure. I'll write it down. Saturday."

"Good. Around seven, okay? My place — I'll cook."

"Sure. Seven is fine. Your place. Great."

He gave me his address, we said our goodbyes, I hung up and waited for my heartbeat to slow down. Dinner at his place? Not that I wasn't ready, but oh my god. Did this mean what I thought it meant?

I'll skip the details of how I got ready for the big date: the body prep — let's just wash those key parts one more time, shall we? — the outfit-choice, makeup, hair, panic attacks, etc., and cut straight to me standing on a sidewalk in the Annex in front of Max's house. It was small, brick, charming, with a wood-framed porch, a peaked roof over a lit second-floor window — the bedroom? I shivered and walked up to the front door.

My hand barely shook when I rang the doorbell, though I did run through one of those routines while I stood there on the porch — Did it ring? It did, right? Or did it? Maybe I should ring again in case I didn't push the button hard enough the first time. But what if it *did* ring, and he's just in the bathroom or somewhere? What if he heard the bell, and he's coming? If he heard it, and he's coming, and I ring again, I'll look impatient. Maybe I'd better wait a minute before I try again. Or has it already been a minute? No, make that an hour.

Just in time, I peered through the glass pane in the door and saw Max coming down a hallway from the back of the house.

He opened the door and said Hi, come on in, and kissed me on the cheek, and I got a whiff of him, mixed up with the aroma of sautéed mushrooms. The Max wave surged through me.

"Come to the kitchen," he said and turned to lead the way. I followed him down the narrow hallway and looked into the small living room — comfy slipcovered couch, worn kilim rug, reading lamp next to a leather chair. Next, the dining room — weathered pine table and chairs, a colourful Central American cloth hanging on the wall. Then the kitchen. I spied the mushrooms, golden brown and sprinkled with fresh herbs, reclining in a copper-bottomed pan on the stove. Next to them, a big stainless steel pot filled with simmering water, homemade pasta coiled alongside. A round wooden table painted azure, set for two, held a small clay pot of baby daffodils.

Max poured me a glass of wine and offered me a basket of thin, homemade cheese straws dusted with paprika, salt, and caraway seeds. I bit into one and let my tongue slide around its soft centre — wonderful. I leaned against the counter. "Your house is lovely, your food is delicious" — I brandished my breadstick — "I feel like I'm in a movie. 'Max's Feast,' we could call it."

Max clinked his glass against mine. "As long as it's not *Rosemary's Baby*." He dropped the pasta into the water, turned up the fire under the mushroom pan, and stirred in some chopped asparagus and roasted orange peppers, a splash of cream. I sipped my wine and salivated at the sight of his arms, exposed in his T-shirt, and at his butt, grabbable in his faded jeans.

Over his shoulder, he said, "You don't mind if we eat right away?"

I put down my glass. "No, that's great. I'm starving." Or I should have been. I'd hardly eaten all day. Only my stomach felt shrunken, tight, like I'd filled up its small space with the breadstick.

He turned toward me and took off his glasses. He took a step closer. "It's great to see you," he said, and slipped his arms around my waist.

I couldn't help it. I grabbed his head and started to neck.

So we break the suction after the big smooch against the counter, and I'm basically ready to abandon all thoughts of food and jump straight into bed, but everything is so ready to serve that, when Max reattaches his glasses and turns back to the stove, I decide to pretend my body is not in a state of full arousal, to go sit at the table, place a napkin on my lap, try to act mature. He brings over two platesful of the most amazing pasta I've ever tasted, and I want to concentrate on the food, except, true to dread, I can't eat much, either of the pasta or of the lovely salad of frisée, Roquefort, toasted hazelnuts, and julienned beet that he serves with it. And when, after a few bites, he leans over and strokes the top of my leg under the table, I drop my fork with a clatter, push my chair closer to his and kiss him and grab his arm and breathe very heavily in his ear until he says, "Maybe we should go upstairs."

We run up the narrow staircase to the attic bedroom, which is lovely — all robin's egg blue walls with white trim and sloping ceilings — where we jump into bed and start rolling around. Things heat up a bit, and he undoes the top few buttons on my dress and kisses the little swell of flesh that's underneath and I'm thinking what a good idea it was to wear the padded push-up tonight so I would *have* swell, except it does occur to me that the problem with these myth-making bras is that the contrast between bra-on and bra-off might be a bit of a shock to someone not acquainted with the current trends in bust-boosting lingerie.

But even I can't dwell on breast-size worries when he's nibbling at my neck, and my hands are inside his shirt, caressing those nice lean shoulders and arms of his. And when, through his trousers and my dress, I can feel something hard and insistent pressing between my legs in a way that makes me remember that my condom-containing purse is downstairs. But no worries, because by the dim light of a small bedside lamp we shrug off our clothes, and he takes out a condom. He flips it on with the sure-handed motions of experience, and we dive under the covers.

The flesh-to-flesh contact is gorgeous — god, it's been ages — and I'm feeling all sorts of crackling and burning sensations throughout, which is all well and good, except there's a certain urgency developing. And it occurs to me as we moan and sigh and kiss and gnaw at each other that what I really need, right now, no more fucking around, is him inside me, the whole enchilada, let's do it.

So I roll us over until he's on top — this is the first time, we can afford to be conventional — and I open my legs and employ all the usual body language to make it more than clear that what's called for here is penetration, no stalling, this level of lubrication does not come around every day, so get in there, and I mean NOW.

And he starts to go in, or tries to go in, but something's awry. He's gone soft, or partly soft. Not completely shrunken and miserable, but soft enough that I'm already mourning the hardness his dick once had, that is, I'll start mourning it as soon as I finish screaming at the top of my lungs from sheer frustration.

No, but really, I'm being quite quiet, a trick I learned from my previous relationship. Yes, despite a level of disappointment that is threatening to spread through my whole body and shut off all sexual response permanently within the next minute, I do not ask what happened, nor do I give a sign that anything is amiss. No, I proceed to go through the motions of intercourse — not an easy task when the dick is practically bending in the middle of each thrust. And the next thing you know — mercifully soon — he's come, and he's out, and I realize how hungry I am. For food.

So we got dressed and went back downstairs and Max reheated the pasta, though not in a microwave, I noticed, but in the sauté pan, like at fancy restaurants with too many waiters who want to interrupt your dinner conversation so you can admire their tableside manner. The dinner was more delicious now that we'd gotten sex out of the way, and then we had dessert — a peach cobbler, no less, with whipped cream — and we started doing this silly licking thing with the cream on the lips and face. Which led to another trip up the stairs to try to connect the male end to the female end in the usual manner, but with the same result. Lots of enthusiasm and the appropriate amount of engorgement during foreplay, then the telltale sag at the crucial moment.

I didn't comment after that second semi-failure, but I couldn't face the thought of trying again, not that night anyway.

Chapter Twenty

Mom gave me a hug. "Hello, sweetheart." She looked behind me. "Are you alone?"

"Max couldn't come. He had to work. His manager called in sick. But he sent a birthday present for Grahame and a cake for us." I hoisted my packages onto the counter. "Hey, Julie, is there any coffee going?"

"You bet."

Mom took cream out of Julie's fridge for me. "That's a shame about Max. Dad and I were looking forward to meeting him."

"Actually, it feels a bit early in the relationship for meeting the parents."

Mom and Julie exchanged a theatrical glance.

"Don't bug me, you guys." I looked over Julie's shoulder at the platter of prosciutto and salami she was arranging. "What should I do?"

Julie pointed at some Styrofoam containers on the kitchen island. "Can you put out the olives?"

"Sure. Where're the kids?"

"Don took them to the park to try out Grahame's new rollerblades. He wants to personally witness the breaking of bones he's positive is going to happen."

Mom lifted a tray full of glasses and cutlery. "I'm going outside to set the table."

I walked over and opened the French doors for her, returned to the counter and opened up containers of olives, herbed feta, and hummus. "How's the painting of that new armoire going?"

Julie slammed the fridge door. "Not."

"What does that mean?"

"Just a second." She carried the meat platter out to Mom, came back in, and closed the door behind her. "Shoot. I almost forgot about the avocados."

She placed three avocados beside a cutting board and started peeling the first. "So I've developed a new theory about life. Want to hear it?"

"Will this explain about the armoire?"

"Yes."

"Okay, go."

"The theory is that everyone has one period in which they shine. Some people have golden childhoods, some are not truly happy or self-fulfilled until they retire. But there's only one 'right' time for everyone. Not more."

I sniffed the beige puréed substance in the latest container I'd opened. "Is this baba ghanouj?"

"Put it out with the pita chips. There, by the phone. Have you been listening to me?"

"Yeah, yeah. One golden time. I'm not sure I recall having had mine. How about you?"

Julie rubbed her nose with the back of her wrist. "But that's just it, don't you see? I had mine twenty-five years ago. Not that I appreciated it then, but that whole cheerleader scene, and going out with Bruce Langford — "

"He was pretty cute."

"He was a total pig. Turned me off sex for months after."

"You slept with him?"

"What I'm trying to say is: that was my time. And it's over now. I'm never going to strike gold again."

"So, what? Don't even try to do something at which you might not succeed? Julie, I want to ask you — have you ever failed at anything?"

Silence while she laid out the avocado, washed her hands, went to the fridge, and took out a container of cut grapefruit sections and a glass bowl containing an orange liquid.

"Julie?" Were those tears in her eyes? "Julie, I'm sorry. That didn't come out right. Look, your stuff is great. Max thinks so, too. All the pieces at my place now are wonderful — some rich parents would pay a mint for that kids' table and chairs. And the green sideboard — if I had a dining room, I'd snap it up immediately."

"Look, I finished the armoire, okay? And I really liked it, I mean, I thought it was maybe the best piece I'd done." Her voice cracked here a little, but she still managed to pick up a bowl and drizzle what appeared to be mango vinaigrette over the avocado and grapefruit in a pattern worthy of a food stylist. "I thought it was so good that I screwed up my courage and mentioned it to the woman who owns that store on Eglinton that specializes in painted furniture. And she came around to take a look. But she didn't like it. In fact, she hated it."

"Are you talking about that place, Rosebuds? The one with the airy-fairy floral crap on breakfast trays? Those dainty vanities? That's not the right place for you. Your work has more energy, more strength — "

Julie held up a hand. "Please stop." She headed outside with the avocado and grapefruit, and I swore to myself I'd find a market for her stuff, no matter what, and prove her stupid theory wrong.

She came back in. "How's it going with Max, anyway?"

"Don't try to change the subject."

Her voice wavered. "Don't you see? Your golden time is still to come. I'm going the other way. And that's the last I'm going to say about this today." She plucked a tissue from the box on the counter and blew her nose. "Now. Tell me about Max."

"What do you want to know?"

"Are you in love, or is it just a fling, or are you getting sick of him already, or what?"

"I don't know. It's okay."

"That's all?"

"No. I like him. A lot. And I think about him all the time and I look forward to seeing him, but there are just some things we have to work out."

"Like what? Religion?"

"No, no. There's no issue there."

"Is it sex, then?"

"Is what sex?"

"Rosemary."

I checked to make sure Mom wasn't heading back in. "Look, have you ever . . . why am I even asking you? The person who's been married for centuries."

"I knew it had to be sex. Go ahead, ask me. I'm more experienced than you might think."

"But you're his friend and everything. He'd kill me if he thought I'd told you."

Mom came into the kitchen. "What about a big pitcher of ice water?" she said.

Julie told Mom where to find a pitcher and handed her some ice cube trays. "So, what are you doing tomorrow?" she said, to me.

"Working at home, probably. Why?"

"Want to go to Body Alive together? We'll do exercise bikes."

"Do I have to?"

She inched over beside me and, under the crashing sound of Mom emptying the ice trays, said, "We can talk about your problem and get some exercise at the same time."

"I don't know. Maybe. I'll call you."

"Believe me, whatever it is, I can solve it."

"Okay," I said to Julie the next morning when we'd settled ourselves on the exercise bikes. A packed aerobics class was jumping up and down on the other side of the glass wall, but we were alone in the cardio room, aside from a lone woman bopping away on the Lifestep to the sounds of her Walkman. "Okay, since when are you a sex thera-pist?"

"Don't you remember that year I spent in Berkeley?"

"No."

She laughed. "I'm kidding. Just tell me what's going on."

Her face was carefree, no sign of yesterday's anguish. "How come you're so cheery today?" I said.

"I started working on a new piece early this morning. It's just an old bookcase I had in Grahame's room, but I couldn't sleep last night, so I got up and started working on it. For fun."

"That's good to hear. But what happened to the one-golden-time theory?"

She took a sip of water. "I don't know. Maybe people get silver and bronze times, too. When you're not glamourous and famous and popular, but life's good enough. *Anyway*, I want to hear about your sex problem. Spare no detail, no matter how gory."

My bike screen showed I was climbing a steep hill. I gripped the handlebars. "Okay. I thought about how I might word this, and here goes. First of all, you must agree in advance that after we've had this conversation, you will erase it from your mind completely and never refer to it, ever."

"Will you just get to it?"

"All right. Now. Here goes. Ahem. Let's say you're making out with a guy —"

"Stop. Define making out. Necking? Petting? Clothes on? Clothes off?"

"Petting? Did you say petting? Does anyone still pet?"

She rolled her eyes and made a cranking motion with her hand.

"Okay. Forget making out. I'm talking foreplay here." I glanced over at the stair-climbing person to see if she might be listening, but even over the whirring of our bike wheels I could hear the tinny sound of her earphone music.

"So. Let's say you're mostly undressed, you're doing pre-inter-course types of things and, well, you just know his dick is hard — "

"How do you know? By touch, by feel, by taste, what?"

"Shit. I don't know. Any of those."

"This is getting gross."

I stopped pedalling. "Forget it. I'm not telling you anything more."

Her legs kept right on pumping, but she laughed. "Who else are you going to ask? Keep talking."

I dropped my shoulders, reprogrammed the bike, and took up the cycling rhythm once more. "Okay. So there you are, and there hasn't been any actual, well, penetration yet, but you know that his dick is hard, that he's perfectly capable of being hard, except when he goes to put it in — "

"It goes droopy."

"How did you know?"

"I told you you were asking the right person. I've been around. I've experienced this."

"With whom?"

"Never mind."

"My sister, the man-eater."

"Anyway, it's not permanent. I mean, probably not. Well, it wasn't when it happened to me."

"Really?"

"It's probably just a confidence thing. Here's some guy face-to-face with a glamourous, desirable woman" — I lifted a hand and made the bullshit sign — "and maybe this guy's a little older, and it's been a while, and he's nervous — your basic performance anxi-ety. So his nervousness goes straight to his penis and, just when he's about to either satisfy you or not — but, he's thinking, more likely not, because you're so experienced with decadent rich Australian sex gods — all his assurance fails him and he droops."

"But he doesn't know about Brian."

No reply from her except heavy breathing.

"Julie? Does he?"

"Well," she said, "I might have mentioned it in passing, months ago, before you two even met. Not that I gave any specifics, just that my little sister was having an affair with an older married man and I was worried about her."

I pedalled on in silence.

"You mad now?"

"No. But how do you make the droop thing stop happening?"

"Time. And lots of stroking." She laughed at the look on my face. "Not that kind. More like telling him you love him, making him feel he has nothing to worry about, that you're not some wanton sex fiend."

"How do you know it's not like Bonnie and Clyde?"

"Bonnie and Clyde?"

"You know how they kept trying to have sex and he couldn't get it up, and she was, like, super-frustrated? When I saw the movie the first time I didn't really get it, but now I'm thinking maybe I should consider giving up on Max. Before I start going out and robbing banks."

"Rosemary. Get a grip. How many times has this happened?"

"Well, it's only been a few weeks, so we've slept together four or five time times now."

"Give it another two weeks to make him feel he has nothing to be afraid of, and if that doesn't work, seek counselling."

"Are you serious?"

"Or maybe a blow job's the answer."

"Julie."

Chapter Twenty-one

"Okay." Phil turned to the sound guys and patted his head. "From the top." The lights went down, the bank of video screens lit up and swirled with the words, *"Panache Presents: Unrequited Love,* and the voice of Fred Astaire floated out through the speakers.

Onto the runway walked Peter, looking suave in Armani and moving like a man who knew his music. What a break he'd turned out to be an aerobics instructor in his spare time. On his arm, matching his gait with her own long-legged happy walk, was Mou-Mou, playing the fiancée, in one of those corny *Sound of Music* alpen-loden outfits.

I sat in the third row beside Phil, the show director. Together, we watched Christine, our first visible-minority face, make her entrance, stage right, in head-to-toe Versace.

"Shit, no," Phil said, softly. "She's coming in too late there."

He stood up, signalled the crew to cut the music, and went to speak to Christine about her timing. I leaned back and yawned. We'd been at this for three hours now, and I was so tense in the shoulders I could tell I'd need a hot bath, a joint, and possibly a glass of cognac before I'd be able to contemplate the idea of sleep. If I ever got home, that is. I looked at my watch. Eight o'clock already, and we were still ironing out the first minute of a ten-minute sequence.

Phil came back and sat down. "Walks like the gawky teenager she is, that Christine. But it's too late to change girls now."

We watched them start over. After a minute, Phil muttered, "For Christ's sake," and stood again, waved his arms. "Back up, back up. Let's try that again, people." He moved up to the first row and lit a cigarette.

Helen walked around from backstage and plopped down beside me.

"Do things look any better from out here?"

"You know what they say: bad dress rehearsal —"

"I know. But now that I've seen the backstage insanity first-hand, I'll never take a show for granted again. Good thing I haven't got anyone important coming to this thing."

"Sean can't make it?"

"No."

"Don't ask?"

She looked grim. "We kind of split up."

"Oh, Helen. What happened? Or can you talk about it?"

"I can talk about it. What happened was that he wasn't Chinese."

"Your parents, you mean?"

"No. They never even met him."

"So?"

She sighed. "He was too out of it. He kept making all these stupid comments, racist comments. Not that he really meant them that way. He wasn't evil or anything. But . . ."

"He just didn't have the faintest comprehension of what your life has been like. Is like. "

"Kind of, yeah."

I tried a smile. "White guys. What can you do?"

"Sean is *so* white, though. He doesn't eat fish or seafood. Or vegetables. Only chicken and beef. And only with potatoes. And he doesn't like rice, says it's too filling."

"Well, why didn't you say so? That explains everything."

She punched me in the arm, lightly. "Look. Over there. You've got company."

Max was standing at the door to the ballroom. I waved him over. "This is a surprise."

"Good surprise?"

I watched him come towards me. "Yeah."

"At least he eats rice," Helen said.

Max sat down on my other side. "Hi, guys. I was in the neighbourhood." He set down a paper shopping bag on the floor, leaned forward in his seat, and watched MouMou pretend to play tennis up on the runway. Peter sat in a group of models doing tennis-spectator motions with their heads, except that Peter's gaze was following the path of a spotlit black model walking by with a briefcase and cellular phone.

"Have you eaten?" Max said.

"Not really."

"Interested in a tomato and goat cheese tart?"

"I am, if she's not," said Helen.

Max reached inside the shopping bag and lifted out a pastry box. He broke the string with his hands, opened the box, and slid out pre-cut slices of tart, one for Helen, one for me. And handed us napkins, too.

We munched away, and talked, and watched Phil go over the staging of the scene, minute by minute.

"What's this supposed to be about?" Max asked.

Helen nudged me. "Tell him, Rosemary."

I gave her a warning look. "Tell him what?"

She laughed. "You should have seen the rationale Rosemary wrote when she proposed this concept. It was pretty funny. But what it's really about is white guys who go for exotic-looking women."

Max frowned.

"Present company excepted, of course," Helen said.

New subject, please. "I spoke to Julie today," I said to Max. "She was feeling discouraged about her painting again. Do you think there's something about the creative process that turns artists into manic-depressives?"

Max patted his pockets. "You know, I almost forgot. A woman came into the shop today and we talked — turns out her best friend is opening up a store downtown that sounds exactly like the kind of place . . . now where did I put that card?" He fished it out of his jeans pocket and handed it to me.

I read it out loud: "Ann Hambleton. Wood Paint."

"The woman said the store's specializing in 'funky painted furniture.' Doesn't that sound like Julie's stuff? Julie should check it out."

Or I could. Without Julie knowing, without raising her hopes. Get this Ann Hambleton over to my place and see if she liked anything before I even mentioned the plan to Julie. That would be the smart thing to do. "Do you mind if I look after this?" I said to Max.

"Not at all." He packed up his bag. "How much longer you think you'll be here?"

"A while. And I have to go back to the office afterwards. Put the jewellery in the vault." I pointed at the heart-shaped diamond pendant MouMou was wearing around her neck.

Helen leaned over. "I can take the jewellery back."

I stood up. "I'll walk you out, Max. Back in a minute, Helen."

We made our way through the empty rows of chairs to the door. "So," I said, "want to come over later?"

"Yeah. What time?"

"Ten. No. Ten-thirty. Is that too late?"

"No." He raised a hand to push my hair back from my face. "Have you ever thought about wearing your hair shorter?"

"You don't like long hair?"

He let his hand fall down to my shoulder and along my arm. "I like you." And the appropriate body parts responded, even though two or three doses of Julie's prescription still hadn't cured our sex problem.

Back at the stage area, I gazed up at MouMou's blissful bride's smile and saw Peter execute a perfect roving eye at the Native wedding photographer. "Thanks for offering to take the jewellery back," I said to Helen. "But I'll do it."

"No. You go see Max. All I'd be doing at home is sitting and brooding."

"So have you sworn off white guys now, or what? Only Chinese men from this day forward?"

Helen smiled. "Hell, no. But I'm thinking of starting out fresh. Moving my base of operations to a new continent. Any suggestions?"

I sigh and roll over, try to get more comfortable, only I can't, because there's something firm and high behind me, something that's definitely not part of my bed. I open my eyes a crack, seeking the comforting red glow of my bedside digital clock. Not there.

I sit up, awake now, eyes wide open, heart galloping. It's okay, Rosemary. Be calm. You're in the living room, your own living room. A throw cushion wet with drool has subbed for a pillow. And a blanket from the linen cupboard that I'd forgotten I owned is half on me, half on the floor.

But where is Max? After the bath and the joint and the cognac, he'd arrived, I recall. And we'd sat down on the couch, and I'd cozied up with my head in his lap and, I guess, fallen asleep.

I walk on bare feet to the bedroom. From the doorway, I hear heavy breathing. I find Max in my bed, the duvet over him, not particularly beautiful in sleep but lovely to look at anyway.

And there's the clock. 4:02. I've slept five hours already. Practically a nightful.

I sit on the edge of the bed, stare at Max sleeping, and reach out to touch his hair. I stroke and smooth, and somehow my touch, which had started out tender, becomes sexual. I let my fingers trail down his neck and into that hollow of the collarbone which is supposed to be such a big bonus-point feature on women, but which seems now, to me, to be a sexy area on men, or specifically on this man, at this moment.

I slip under the duvet and slide into spoon position behind Max. I cuddle up to him, feeling that drowsy warmth I felt the first time we kissed on my front porch. Asleep still, he does not react to my spooning and sighing, except to shift his weight and make a wet sort of sound with his lips, like he's eating something small and delicate and tasty in his dreams.

I'm rapidly getting in the mood for eating something tasty, though not necessarily small and delicate, myself. I press against him and am rewarded, when I move my hand down, with the feel of a good, solid erection.

He moans when I stroke him and turns over on his back. And the idea forms in my mind that this could be it. My big chance. I start devising a plan. I'll have to proceed with extreme caution to make this work. And the damn condom will be a problem, for sure. I consider — only for a few seconds — going bare. But no, I don't need to risk it, when patience is all that's required here, and a steady hand. Not that I've ever been good at patience, and especially not when my erogenous zones are limbering up for the big workout. Smart thinker that I am, I leave the room to whip off my PJs and rip open the condom package. I tiptoe back into the room, condom in hand, lower myself onto the bed, and bite my lip and fold down the duvet, pausing between movements, anything not to startle him.

With only a few sleepy murmurs from Max, I manage to pull the condom on, and down, and the erection is still with us, in strength, bobbing up like a buoy in a choppy sea. Yes.

I stretch a leg over, pinning him down so he won't roll back onto his side. I position myself on hands and knees above him and reach back. I check my own equipment. All systems go. I line up tab A with slot B and make the insertion. Ooh. Aah.

He begins to wake, though his eyes stay closed. He moans in a way that makes me crazy, and his hands reach up for me. I tense for a moment, afraid even semi-consciousness may cause a decline, but we've got a pretty hot lick going here and he's dancing right along, in the groove.

His moans get louder, more intense, and I join in with a few sounds of my own, for the hell of it, to keep him company.

Later, when it was all over, after we'd wakened the neighbourhood with our cries, after we'd disentangled ourselves and used up an entire box of tissues wiping away excess fluids, Max reached over and hugged me and whispered, "I love you, Rosemary."

And if I weren't such a shy, retiring type, I might have said the same.

Chapter Twenty-two

I'd meant to be in early to work the next day, the day of the gala, but after Max and I had fallen back asleep, it had been a struggle to wake up when the clock radio turned on at seven, and then Max had felt a need to demonstrate that his middle-of-the-night performance had not been a fluke. Very convincing he was, too, only by the time he'd proved his facility (bolstered not a little by that airing of the L-word), no way could I hit the office until nine-twenty, and that was with a ton of mad rushing.

I sat down at my desk, and without even touching my coffee I pulled Ann Hambleton's card from my purse and dialled the number. It rang, I eased the lid off my cup, and noticed a pink message slip, placed in the exact centre of my desk blotter, from Helen. "CALL ME BEFORE YOU DO ANYTHING!" the message said. The Urgent box had been ticked four times.

"Ann Hambleton here," said a voice.

I talked fast, introduced myself, mentioned Julie and the painted furniture, dropped Max's name. Helen walked into my office, mimed something that looked like, "Finally, you show up!" and started making cutting motions with her hand on her neck, but I shook my head, pointed to the phone, and listened to what Ann Hambleton was saying, which was, "Your sister's work sounds exactly like the sort of thing I had in mind for my shop, but I'm a little frantic at the moment, because I'm flying off tomorrow morning on a buying trip. Could I call you when I get back?"

"Oh. Sure. Only I'd been hoping to . . . but . . . of course. Whatever you say."

She hesitated. "Unless I could see you late this afternoon. One of my appointments just cancelled. Is that possible?"

"Today?"

Helen started making like she was strangling herself, complete with choking noises. I stifled a laugh, opened my book, and looked at my schedule, which, while crazy re: the gala, did have a certain four-to-five-o'clock slot already marked, "Go home and change."

I arranged for Ann Hambleton to come by my place at four-thirty, and I got off the phone.

"Can I talk now?" Helen said.

"What? What?"

She closed my door. "I was going to call you at home with this scoop last night, but it was late, and I didn't want to interrupt anything . . ." She winked.

I sipped my coffee. "You're in a good mood."

"This? This is not a good mood. This is hysteria. Okay, ready?"

"Ready."

"Cast your mind back to last night. You go off to meet Max, I head up to the office with the stupid jewellery. It's about ten o'clock, and I'm getting tired."

Helen's cab had driven up to the MacKenzie building, and she was filling out the chit in the back seat when the driver said, "Looks like I've got my next fare."

Helen looked through the windshield and saw Elizabeth Crowley standing with a group of suited men on the sidewalk, one arm raised to flag the cab. She got out of the car, said Hi to Elizabeth. Elizabeth started, stopped, said Hello, looked back at the men dispersing on the sidewalk, and bolted into the cab.

"Have we come to the good part yet?" I said.

"Stop it. Listen. So I go inside and I sign in with security, but just as the guard comes around the desk to unlock the elevator, his phone rings, and he starts talking to his supervisor."

Helen is standing there with the heavy box of jewellery and her briefcase and her purse, getting a little pissed-off, when her eye is caught by the sign-in binder, sitting on the desk. Which she realizes has a sign-*out* section on the left-hand side of the page. She scans the page, recognizes Elizabeth's scrawl, reads the names of some Mac-Kenzie Communications ultra-bigwigs, and—"I couldn't believe it. The last entry was — and the more I think about it, I more I see how everything falls into place, now that I know. Because the last entry on the page was — "

My phone rang, Elizabeth Crowley's extension showing on the screen. I laughed and held a finger up to Helen. "Rosemary McKinnon."

"Hello, Rosie. Brian Turnbull here."

Wild-eyed, I looked over at Helen. "Brian? But my phone says — what are you doing here?"

Helen slapped her head, rolled her eyes, grabbed a piece of notepaper and started writing.

"I'll explain later," Brian said, while I read Helen's note: Did you already know? Know what? I wrote back.

"I think we should meet somewhere, for a cup of tea," Brian said. "How about coffee?"

Helen passed me her next note: He was with E.C. last night!

I shook my head, not getting it, and answered Brian. "Okay. Sure. Five minutes. The coffee place on the corner. See you there."

"Oh, and Rosie."

Helen was shoving the paper so close to my face I couldn't read it. "What?" I said, to both of them.

"Don't tell anyone you're meeting me."

"Fine, goodbye." I hung up the phone and tried to read Helen's last note. " 'He owns this place.' Is that what this says? What does it mean?"

Helen came around the desk and grabbed me by the shoulders. "Rosemary, don't you see? There's only one explanation. He's bought the company."

"Don't be ridiculous. Why would he do that?"

Helen let go of me. "I think I need to lie down."

I whipped out a brush and ran it through my hair. "Stay calm. I'll be back in half an hour with an explanation for everything."

I left her sitting in my office, head down on my desk.

"You look lovely," was his opener. "Glowing." He reached over and touched my hair.

This guy, with his moves and his lines. "You've cut your hair," I said.

Instead of the collar-brushing locks he'd once sported, now the back of his hair was closely cropped. Only the top stayed long and wavy. "Looks good."

"You haven't," he said.

"Haven't what?"

"Cut your hair."

"No, but I'm thinking of doing it real soon. Something like yours, actually. Long on the top, shaved at the back. I might even get some words carved in the hair at the base of my skull, right here." I bent my head over the table and pointed. "Have it say 'Fashion Victim,' maybe. What do you think?"

His cellular phone rang. "Damn," he said, and turned off the ringer. "Look, I don't have much time. But I wanted to speak to you privately before the news gets out."

"What news? Helen thinks you bought *Panache*. Funny, eh?"

"Actually, I bought MacKenzie Communications. A friendly takeover."

"You're kidding."

He grinned.

"You're not kidding. Why?"

"MacKenzie is a good fit with my other holdings. It's a matter of global economies, and a foothold in the North American market —" He cut himself off. Must have seen my eyes glazing over. "At any rate, I've been working on this deal for two years, and now it's done."

He pushed his untouched tea aside and leaned forward on the table. "This is strictly confidential. No one's to know until tomorrow. My people are working right now with the MacKenzie staff preparing the press releases and the memos to staff. The usual assurances that business will proceed as usual. But I wanted to tell you now, beforehand."

"Let me get this straight. Are you saying that, in effect, you are now my boss? Hah!"

"We'll discuss your career another time. Just remember: be quiet about what I've told you."

I laughed, nice and hollow. "You don't actually expect me to do what you say, do you?"

His eyes did an angry look, but I wasn't scared. "Until tonight, then," he said, and stood up, pulled back his jacket and dug into his pocket.

Tonight? What, tonight? I stared at the white of his shirtfront, saw how it tucked into the slim waist of his slate blue trousers, watched his tanned hand count out three loonies and place them on the table.

He was leaving. I jumped up, grabbed my bag and followed him out. "What do you mean, tonight? You calling a staff meeting?"

He turned back, showed me his profile. "Chloe and I will be at the benefit tonight. We support the philanthropic efforts of my publications whenever we can."

Chloe was in town? How wonderful. And how cozy we'd all be tonight, meeting and greeting, sitting down, enjoying the show . . .

I stopped short. Oh god. Unrequited Love.

The image popped into my head of Peter and MouMou cavorting onstage while their real-life counterparts watched from the floor. Aaagh! Maybe I should warn Brian. Beg him to stay home or come late. Maybe I should apologize in advance, or better still, tell him I had nothing to do with it.

But before I was able to choose from among these enticing options, he had gone.

Quietly, now, indeed. I called Helen into my office as soon as I got back.

"Did I tell you?" she said. "I told you."

"Business as usual, my ass. If he thinks I'm going to work for him, he can forget it."

Helen stared off. "What about Elizabeth, though? Why did she look so guilty last night? It must have been because my name's at the top of the hit list. I should have caught wind of this before now. I should have started my job search months ago."

"Who made him king? That's what I want to know."

"You still haven't gotten over him, have you?"

"I have too."

"Wanna bet? How'd he look today? Tell me."

"He's cut his hair, very stylish — it made him look younger. And he was wearing this suit of a very fine dark blue wool, almost an exact match for his eyes, and — oh, shut up."

"It's okay. I haven't gotten over Sean yet either. But hey, what about Max? How's he going to feel about Brian being on the scene?"

"Max?"

"You remember Max."

"Tell me this is all a bad dream."

"And then there's the show to do."

I groaned.

Helen pushed herself up from the chair. "And what a show it will be."

Somehow, between us, Helen and I took care of all the tasks to be done that day, and I even made it home almost on time, so I had a whole fifteen minutes to tidy up before Ann Hambleton came over. A good thing, too, because the blanket I'd slept under on the couch was still draped halfway onto the floor, and clothes were strewn about on almost every piece of Julie's furniture. I whisked them away and just managed to complete some whirlwind dusting before I let Ann in the front door.

"Thanks for coming," I said.

"You're very welcome." She looked around my living room. "These must be the things here, are they? Could you give me a few minutes?"

"Sure, no problem." She turned her back to examine a coffee table, and I checked her out. She was a bit hippie-ish, but upscale hippie — her purple suede Birkenstocks looked new, and her Indian-print dress was made of a beautiful silk. Which appearance seemed more promising than not. I mean, if she'd come in looking like a real estate agent in an aggressive red wool suit, I might have expected her not to like Julie's stuff. But hell, what did I know.

I watched her open a dresser drawer and I remembered I was supposed to be getting ready — I had to be downtown in an hour. I slipped into my bedroom, unearthed the dress I planned to wear, and started digging in my drawer for my best pair of sheer pantyhose.

"Excuse me," she said, and I popped out of my bedroom and into the living room.

"Now am I to understand that these pieces are your sister's work, and you represent your sister?"

"Well, yeah. I mean, actually I work for a magazine. But in this instance, I guess I represent her. So, yes to your question."

She studied me. "A magazine. Really. Which one?"

"*Panache*. I'm the fashion editor. Well, for now I am."

She sat down on the arm of my couch. "Is that so? And how long have you worked there?"

"Too long. Ten years."

"You must have made a lot of contacts in that time."

"Yeah, well. For a big city, Toronto's a small town."

"Hmmm." She stood up and ran her finger along the surface of the child's table. "Well, I'm definitely interested in these pieces. But I wonder if . . . do you have a few minutes? Let's see what we can work out."

I moved my glass around on the table, making wet circle marks on the fake marble surface. "I wish I still smoked. I could really get into a cigarette right now."

Helen leaned back on the banquette. "I wish I could drink without becoming red-faced and obnoxious after only one."

"Uh oh. Don't look. Two guys at the bar are giving us the eye."

She looked. "They're smiling at me and nodding," she said, with clenched teeth.

The thing was, we *were* wearing attention-getting clothes. Helen had on a black slipdress, mini, and I'd donned a long-sleeved metallic silver number. And we both sported high heels, serious hose, and done hair and makeup — all for the gala, which was black tie, after all, but we'd ended up being ready ahead of time, and I'd told Helen if we didn't get out of the ballroom I might scream, so we'd retreated to the hotel bar for a quick one.

The waiter brought over refills of our drinks: one soda water, one Coke. "Compliments of the two gentlemen at the bar," he said. We looked, they waved.

"Shit," I said. "Let's get out of here."

"Hey." Helen sat up straighter. "I meant to tell you: I watched this old Fred Astaire movie on TV last night, on the late show. It was about a Russian babe who wore these form-fitting jersey wrap dresses. Do you know the movie I mean?"

"*Silk Stockings*. That was Cyd Charisse."

"Oh. Well, anyway, in this scene near the end, she wears a circle skirt and dances with these Cossacks."

"I used to dream about that skirt. The way it twirled when she spun. The way the fabric lifted and arranged itself in folds going the same direction as her turns. Wasn't it great?"

Helen drank some Coke. "You've seen this movie a few times."

"A few."

"Well, yeah, the skirt *was* great, and I know you like Fred Astaire — he was pretty smooth, though he looked fairly ancient — but the rest of the movie was so . . . so . . ."

"Romantic?"

"No. Sick. I mean, here this woman is supposed to be oppressed and frigid because she's devoted too much of her life to work. And only when she discovers the joys of lingerie is she able to orgasm."

"You know, it's been a while since I saw it, but I can't quite bring the orgasm scene to mind. What was she wearing in that one?"

"The attitudes were just so oppressive, so fifties, so anti-feminist, I don't know how you can — oh, no. Here's Marni."

Marni slid into the booth. "Hi. I'm glad I found you. There's something I have to tell you, Rosemary."

Helen started to get up. "I'm going to the washroom."

Marni blocked Helen's way out. "No, stay. You'll find out soon enough anyway." Helen sat back down. "Now. You both know about the sale of MacKenzie Communications to Brian Turnbull, right?"

"Well, we, that is . . ."

"They say our jobs will be secure, but we know what that means — a clean sweep within a year."

Helen and I exchanged glum glances.

"I was upset about it at first, too. But maybe it's for the best. It's probably time for all of us to move on. Time for me to get out of there, for sure. So I've taken a pre-emptive strike. I've accepted another job offer and I'm leaving *Panache* at the end of the month."

Helen and I both spoke at once. "Really?" "For where?"

"I'll be working for the Fashion Network. Anchoring a new series they're developing on what goes on behind the scenes. Not publicity puff pieces for the designers, more of a documentary approach. Warts and all."

"Well, congratulations, Marni," I said. "Good for you." Helen said something similar.

"Now, Rosemary," Marni said. "It seems that I owe you an apology."

Helen stood up. "You know what? I really do have to go. Excuse me." She edged out of the booth and walked to the can past the stares of the men at the bar.

"Look, Marni," I said, "I guess I've been feeling a little burnt-out lately, and —"

"Let me talk. I know you saw me that day at Perfecto with Greg Smithfield, and I know what you must have thought. And it was true — he was also thinking of buying the company, and he met with me to try to get some inside information."

"I thought you were interviewing for a job."

"Well, he owns the Fashion Network, so that worked out in the end, but that's not why we initially met, no."

I sat, remembering.

"But the reason Greg didn't pursue buying MacKenzie was because he found out there was a competing bid from someone willing to pay more. From Brian Turnbull. We knew he had to have someone on the inside, and I mistakenly believed that you were that person."

"Me?"

"You two seemed awfully chummy. And when we travelled, you kept disappearing anytime he and you were in the same city. For clandestine meetings, I thought." She looked me in the eye. "But I guess I was wrong."

I met her gaze. "I guess."

"So. I'm sorry."

"Well, I'm sorry, too. If I've been testy lately. Nothing to do with this deal, seeing as it's all news to me. I guess I've just been feeling a certain lack of motivation."

"Well, how does the thought of TV motivate you? I can't promise anything yet, but it's a whole new show, we'll have to hire staff — you could put your journalism training to use. And frankly, I'd like to have someone bright and competent around, someone I can trust."

"Think about it," she said, and stood up to let Helen back in. "And I think you should both know that Elizabeth Crowley was the person Brian had planted among us."

"So that's why she looked so guilty last night," Helen said.

"How do you know?" I asked Marni.

Marni smiled her old, cold, bitchy smile. "Who do you think will be announced tomorrow as the vice-president in charge of publishing for all of MacKenzie Communications?"

"Excuse me," said a male voice. The two men from the bar were standing there. They'd sucked in their stomachs and wore smarmy grins on their faces. "We're from out of town, and we're wondering if you girls might know of a place to get some good Chinese food around here."

Marni looked them up and down. "There's a marvellous buffet across the road, in the Continental Hotel. You'll enjoy it." She turned back to us. "Let's go, ladies. The party awaits."

The two guys backed off, but not before I heard one say to the other, "I told you they were call girls."

7:00 - 8:00 p.m. Cocktails. During the cocktail hour, I was supposed to greet guests at the door, schmooze, make people feel warm and welcome for their $250-a-head, and look glamourous. Right.

Granted, the silver sheath I wore was divinely chic and well-cut — it didn't make me look fat, flat, or short — but it did lack one key quality I usually like in clothes — the ability to breathe. As in: you wear synthetic fabrics in high-stress, bright-light situations and guess what happens. Sweat. And it was one of those deals where the wetter I felt the fabric under my arms getting, the more I sweated. With the increasing certainty that lifting the arms at all, that doing anything, in fact, other than keeping them pinned to the sides, would be a major mistake.

Add to the sweat problem that I'm not a natural schmoozer on normal, calm days, let alone on a day during which I learned my job was in jeopardy, was sort of offered another, *and* had my ex-lover drop in and touch my hair in a coffee shop. The capper being that I could look forward to meeting his wife real soon.

Oh great. There was Brian now. I watched him shake hands and nod to Elizabeth as if they hadn't been in deep cahoots for the last year — good faking, guys. And I tried not to notice how his tuxedo seemed to have been designed for the sole purpose of showcasing his physique.

But I couldn't not notice Chloe Turnbull. Blonde and fair, and wearing an awful flapper-style dress. Brian introduced us. I said Hello though a forced smile and focused on something behind her ear just to stop myself from giving her a once-over to end all once-overs, from her caplike hair to her satin pumps. Satin pumps? How outré, when all the hip chicks had on strappy high-heeled black suede or silver patent Manolo Blahniks.

Brian was already turned away, talking to Carolyn, who was carrying a black lace fan to go with the latest in the long line of black lace dresses she seemed to possess.

Chloe shook my hand and spoke in a posh English accent. "What a smashing dress you're wearing! I must say I feel a little dowdy in mine — it was my grandmother's."

And it looked it, too. I noticed the intricate sequin work on the vintage silk. "Beautiful beading," I said.

She glanced around and lowered her voice. "I didn't realize Toronto would be quite so trendy." Her worried eyes searched out Brian's face.

And guess what. I felt sorry for her. Because she wasn't perfect. That dress, the shoes, the fact that her nose was a little on the long side. And because I could imagine what being married to Brian would be like — all that intensity, the way he never ate. Not to mention his roving eye. Even now he stood, not ten paces away, laughing while Carolyn told him a story that required her to tap him on his tuxedoed pecs with that dumb fan.

"Listen," I said, "You're just the only person here confident enough to wear something original." I touched the skirt of my silver dress. "The rest of are mere slaves to fashion."

"Thank you," she said. "It's sweet of you to say so." She looked at a slip of paper she held in her hand. "Would you know where table number two might be?"

I gave her directions, turned to greet the next person, and prayed Chloe wouldn't recognize herself in MouMou during the Unrequited Love segment. After all, there were tons of differences — MouMou was thinner, taller, had a surgically enhanced perfect nose. And wore dowdy clothes in every set-up. Help me.

Julie and Don came through the ballroom doors. Don pointed at my dress. "Next time we run out of aluminum foil, can I call you?"

"Don't listen to him," Julie said. "Your dress is lovely. How are you? Nervous?"

"Can you see the sweat stains?" I lifted my arms an inch.

"No, just a little wrinkling. Really. It's fine. Oh. You left me a message to call you?"

"Yeah. I've got good news, but I can't tell you now. Later."

She leaned in close. "Is it about Max? You know, the problem?"

I laughed. "No. Well, yes and no. Way too much has happened today. Where are you sitting?"

Julie turned to Don. "Where are we sitting?" To me she said, "I know we're with Max and whoever else is at table number —"

Don retrieved their slip of paper. "Two. Table two."

I grabbed the slip from his hand. "Let me see that. Oh my god. You're sitting with Brian Turnbull and his new wife."

Julie's face lit up. "Really? Why is he here? Oh, I get to meet him at last. What fun."

"And Max is sitting there too? This is going to be one swell evening."

"Don't worry," Julie said. "I'll handle everything."

Don looked perplexed. "But isn't Turnbull the guy who Rosemary — "

"Come along, dear," Julie said, "and pay attention now, while I explain."

8:00 - 9:00. Dinner Service. Dinner? Hah. First of all, I wouldn't touch it — after all, it was hotel food for five hundred. And whenever I see a phoney-looking engraved menu which includes among its calligraphically listed courses sherried consommé, potatoes parisienne (like those little freeze-dried puffs are supposed to be higher up on the food scale than mashed), and a dessert that contains components both flambéed and frozen, I plan to eat elsewhere.

Not that I had the chance to eat, what with last-minute backstage conferences with Phil, who informed me he had replaced Christine the model with someone named Yasmin. "Don't worry," he said. "Yasmin will be fine. I went over everything with her this afternoon and it's going to go like clockwork. I swear."

I considered adding this news to my list of things to sweat about but decided not to bother with anything so trivial when I could spend productive mind time instead doing what I'd been doing every other minute for the whole day: foreseeing the acute embarrassment I would suffer when my adolescent revenge fantasies were exposed to everyone I know and hold dear. And to everyone I hold not dear.

I flitted about from table to table. At mine, it was:

"So Marni, when are you going to hand in your resignation? You already did? How did Elizabeth take it? You're kidding. A severance?"

At table two, I hardly knew who to approach first. "Max, hi." I kissed him on the cheek — a platonic public kiss. "When did you get here? Nice tuxedo. Me? Oh, thanks, but it's so hot in here. In the dress, I mean. Speedy? Yeah, I guess I am. It's been a crazy day."

I smiled a hysterical smile at Brian, Chloe, and Don. "Julie, I wonder if I could get you to help me backstage for a second."

Julie stood up and followed me away from the table, nattering in my ear. "What a group. That Brian is certainly smooth and handsome, but a little old for the young wife, don't you think? She's a sweet thing but not too bright. Why he picked her over you I'll never know. He seemed quite interested to hear I was your sister, though. Started asking me questions that were making Max listen rather closely — did I sail, was I a journalist also. But when I asked him what had brought him to town, that sure shut him up. Why is he here?"

I'd pulled Julie behind a screened-off area at the base of the runway where the sound equipment was set up — the crew were off finishing dinner. "I don't have time to tell you everything now. But here's the best news: I sold some of your furniture today."

"What? How?"

I explained about Max and his customer and Ann Hambleton and the viewing. "So she wants to take everything! She'll pay outright for the armoire and the children's table, and the rest on consignment. And keep it coming! she said. Isn't that great?"

Julie hugged me. "Oh, Rosemary."

"Anyway, I thought I should tell you now, before the shit hits the fan."

"What shit? What fan?"

The sound guys had returned and were checking levels and murmuring into their headsets.

"We'd better go."

We walked back to our tables and I slid into my seat next to Helen.

"Thank you all so much for coming," the master of ceremonies said, "and welcome." He started in on a speech about the opera company.

I whispered to Helen. "I think I'm going to have a nervous breakdown."

"Then I won't tell you that the dress MouMou wears in the third set-up ripped right down the back, *not* on the seam."

Marni leaned over and shushed us.

"And now," said the emcee, "sit back and enjoy the show."

Sure thing.

9:00 - 9:45. Evening Wear Presentation. This part of the show, the main part, had nothing to do with us. So I could sit there and pretend to watch the models without paying any attention at all. I put on the noncommittal mask I wear when viewing clothes and took stock of my physical symptoms. Surely a racing pulse combined with a stomach squeezed into a tight knot, a face so heated it could have grilled cheese sandwiches, and a leg that wouldn't stop jiggling might collaboratively produce a spectacular effect like a stroke or an aneurysm. Or less spectacular, but with its own dramatic cachet — another fainting spell.

I took gulps from my glass of ice water and wished the waiters hadn't taken away the bread baskets — I could have used a nice crusty roll right then, or even one of the white spongy ones the hotel had offered.

But in no time the first part of the show was over. All the models came out and posed onstage in their ballgowns and cocktail frocks, and my heartbeat pumped up the volume until its boom threatened to drown out the sound of applause in my ears.

9:45. Show Finale. "And now," the disembodied announcer's voice boomed out, "*Panache* magazine presents . . . Unrequited Love!" The title came up on the video screens, Helen reached over and squeezed my hand, Fred Astaire started to sing, and Peter walked out on stage with MouMou on his arm. They bopped along like happy lovebirds and I watched, my breath held, my sweat still.

When they reached the end of the runway, Peter knelt down on one knee in front of MouMou and flourished a blue velvet ring box. MouMou slipped on the ring, gasped with delight, and pulled Peter to his feet for a big hug.

The audience clapped and chuckled. I checked the heads around and in front of me. Elizabeth's was tilted to one side, a proud smile on her face. Marni stared into the void, visualizing herself in a TV studio far away from here. Helen scrutinized the action, looking for screw-ups. At table two, Julie was smiling, Max looked pensive, and I saw Brian lean over toward Chloe and whisper something in her ear.

And damn if she didn't then turn around, seek me out, and send me a big smile. Thereby missing the tableau of MouMou, preoccupied by the huge diamond on her finger, and Peter, doing a very big over-the-shoulder leer at slinky Yasmin. The audience laughed loudly, and sweat resumed its steady flow down my sides.

It was going to be a long ten minutes.

Chapter Twenty-three

I kicked off the high heels, stretched my aching toes, threw my shoes on the passenger seat, and started the car with a stocking foot on the gas pedal.

I drove around the fifth level of the parking lot and down a spiral ramp. Around and around. And around. I was so tired my eyeballs stung, though the excessive amount of makeup I was wearing sure didn't help. What I needed to do, and soon, was to get home and rip off the infernal dress, not to mention everything underneath it. All those seams and elastic and spandex and nylon on my skin were making me want to scratch everywhere.

I'd pull on a soft T-shirt and a pair of baggy knit shorts. I'd run into the bathroom, pull my hair back from my forehead with a cheap nylon hairband, and apply gobs of Vaseline to my eyes. I'd wipe off the makeup with a tissue and be rewarded by the sight of industrial-strength tar smears on the Kleenex. Aah. Couldn't wait. I braked, took my place in the line of cars waiting to pay the cashier, and re-lived the past half-hour in living colour.

So maybe the whole Unrequited Love idea was majorly imma-ture, but Peter and MouMou, I gotta tell you, looked perfect when they walked down the runway as bride and groom.

MouMou wore a sleeveless Laura Ashley wedding dress — all white eyelet and empire waist, with tiny lilac sprigs in her hair — and there was something about her paleness and those long anorexic arms. She looked the picture of the storybook bride.

Peter, meanwhile, was in white tie — an oblique reference to Fred Astaire, though Peter wasn't quite skinny enough in the waist or butt to really show a white vest and tails off to maximum effect. Just as well, though, that he wasn't in a tuxedo, so his resemblance to Brian wouldn't seem so marked.

Or was I the only one twisted enough to have seen the tenuous connection between Peter and Brian? Because afterwards, when it was all over and everyone was up and saying goodbye, no one let on they'd noticed any twinlike qualities. Not to me, anyway.

Not Helen, who shook my hand, and said, "See? Without a hitch. But we weren't worried, right? I'm out of here."

Or Julie. "Congratulations! Where *do* you come up with these ideas? I have to run — the babysitter's waiting. But I'll call you tomorrow. And thanks so much about my stuff. I'm really excited about it."

Or Marni. "I thought it went well, Rosemary. And let's talk, soon."

Max next. "I see there's more than one creative force in your family."

"You're teasing me."

"No, it was original, your story — and surprising. A little twisted, mind you. But funny."

"That's me, twisted."

He took my hand in his. "So. What are you doing now?"

"Oh, Max, I'm such a wreck. I think we'd better not." I spotted Brian over Max's shoulder, waiting. To speak to me? Gulp. And was that a glower in his eyes?

Max looked back at Brian, then at me, eyes narrowed behind his glasses.

"Sorry," I said. "Do you mind?"

He picked a piece of something off my shoulder. "I'll call you." He walked away.

Brian and Chloe stepped up. "Rosemary," she said, "what a finale! It was like a little play! Very entertaining."

Relief. She hadn't recognized herself.

She turned to Brian. "Didn't you think it was clever, darling?"

"Quite clever, yes. I'm curious, though, as to what inspired you to come up with that concept. If you don't mind my asking."

I was ready for this. "You know what happened? I was cleaning out a closet, and inside a box of my old high school things I found an ancient tab of acid, burnt into a little square of pink blotting paper — do you know the type?" Brian looked sceptical, Chloe blank. "So, anyway, I dropped it for old times' sake, and the next thing you know" — I snapped my fingers — "Unrequited Love."

Brian grunted. Chloe said, "I don't understand."

"I'm sorry. I was joking. About taking LSD. You know, the drug? Actually, the tab I found had lost all its potency — expired, I guess. I'm afraid that in real life, my ideas are merely the product of a fevered brain."

"Well," she said, "it was lovely meeting you, anyway."

Brian had given me one of his enigma faces, and they'd left.

I zoomed up Jarvis and cut through Rosedale over to Yonge Street, to my neighbourhood.

I'd have to call Max as soon as I got home and explain about Brian. Or not explain, but tell him . . . tell him . . .

Okay. So maybe Max didn't look as good in a tux as some people, maybe he wasn't big and strong, but he'd come along, and whenever I thought of him, there was this whole rose-blooming-in-time-lapse-photography thing going on in my heart area. Which seemed an awful lot like love to me.

I let all the evening's turmoil fly away from my head and wallowed in mind-pictures of Max and me lying in bed, bodies intertwined, sleepily talking; of Max and me eating —

Stop the gooey montage, already. I hadn't eaten anything since lunch. And that unsettled feeling in my stomach wasn't nerves left over from the show, it was hunger.

The clock on the dashboard read 10:35. The Chinese greasy spoon around the corner from my house stayed open until eleven. I'd just make it.

So there I was, sitting on the couch in T-shirt and baggy shorts, hair sticking up in an ugly hairband, stomach protruding from ingestion of vast quantities of tofu and greens on rice, hold the MSG, fried wonton on the side. The mug of herbal tea in one hand, the TV remote in the other. It was midnight and I still couldn't sleep, even after having spent the previous half-hour flinging the love phrase back and forth through the phone lines with Max.

So I'm channel-flipping and waiting for the nervous system to figure out that the sun went down hours ago and we can go to sleep now, when my doorbell rings.

Kind of an unsettling thing to happen when you're alone in your apartment late at night and you're not expecting anyone. After I told myself that it probably wasn't a homicidal maniac — why ring? — it occurred to me that it might be Max, come by for a surprise visit. I flipped off my hairband, shook up my hair, slid up to the front door, and peeked through the spyhole. To see, not Max, but Brian. Standing sideways with his ear to the door.

"Rosie?" he whispered loudly.

I mouthed the word fuck and leaned with my back against the door. For a second, I contemplated standing there, not breathing, until I heard him walk away.

To hell with it. I opened the door. "So you're pissed off because of that Unrequited Love thing. I'm sorry, okay? It was a dumb thing to do. But how was I to know you'd buy the company and show up tonight?"

He stood on the doorstep, polo-shirt collar turned up, hands in his jeans pockets, looking handsome and virile and like a movie star. "May I come in?"

I sat down on my couch. He looked around. "Interesting furniture."

"I'm just storing this stuff. They're my sister's work. They're all sold."

He bent over and examined the dresser top more closely, then straightened up and moved in front of the fireplace, hands still in pockets. He looked out of place in my living room, like he was too tall for the ceiling. Or too formal for the clothes-on-the-floor, take-out-containers-on-the-coffee-table decor.

"Oh, sit down." I gestured to a painted child's chair which, while sturdy enough to hold his weight, would not necessarily be comfortable.

He stayed standing. "The sister who painted these is the one I met tonight? The attractive, outgoing blonde?"

"Yeah, her. Hard to believe we're related, I know." I walked over to the window, lifted a slat of blind, and peered out into the night. "How'd you get here, anyway?"

"I had a car bring me over. The driver's waiting outside."

Sure enough, there was a long black car parked across the street, lights out. I could barely discern the profile of a man sitting behind the steering wheel.

"And where does Chloe think you are?" I picked up the food containers and carried them into the kitchen.

"She quite liked you, you know," Brian called from the other room.

"Weird, eh?" I came back in and sat down.

He was silent. Probably counting to ten. "Rosie, I want to explain some things."

Like how it was time for me to look for another job. "Go ahead. I can take it."

He started pacing around my living room, which was not an easy thing to do, what with Julie's furniture cluttering up the joint.

"Look," he said, "I know you're probably thinking that I only approached you in the first place because I was working on the deal to acquire MacKenzie, and, to some extent, that's true."

"You mean it wasn't because of my slanted beaver?"

He stopped pacing. "I beg your pardon?"

I pulled my legs up under me and started waving my hands around. I was blushing now, but so what. "Just tell me straight out. Do you have a thing for exotic women or not? Do non-white women, as a concept, turn you on? Yes or no. And don't bullshit me."

He sat down on one of Julie's chairs. "I don't . . . look, I . . ."

"So it's yes. Admit it."

"I still find you very attractive, if that's what you want to know."

Uh oh. My crotch area started doing this throb-and-heat action, like a furnace kicking on when the thermostat hits the pre-set temperature. I willed it to cool down and reminded myself that I was already involved with someone who loved *me*, not my type. "Look, I always thought that you, well, that you were attracted to me because . . . that it was the ethnic thing. You know. Oriental flower and all that crap."

"I knew you thought that. All I can say is that I first went after you for business reasons."

I slouched down on the couch. "Why is this not any better than the slanted beaver theory?"

He came over and sat on the coffee table facing me, his knees touching mine. He reached out and took my hands. "But it became more than that. You and I could never get on permanently — you're too strong for me, and independent, and bright. But it was marvellous while it lasted, our affair. I only ended it because Marni became suspicious, and the deal was coming close to being completed, and I didn't want you involved."

I withdrew my hands. "And because of Chloe?"

"Yes, well, that too. But I didn't want you to think, when you found out about the take-over, that our time together had only been about business."

His hand went up to my hair like he was going to touch it, but I stopped him, partly because I knew that running the fingers through the mane at that point in the evening would not have been a pleasant experience, considering that the ten pounds of mousse and spray I'd applied earlier had turned my normally silky locks into something that felt like clumps of straw.

"So you weren't pissed off about the Unrequited Love thing?"

"I laughed when I first saw the concept in your book. The joke was on me, rather, wasn't it? Though it was Elizabeth's idea to execute the story, not mine. She saw it as a way to make a splash."

"What do you mean, when you saw my book?"

"Who do you think commissioned it? I'd asked Elizabeth to have her senior people put some proposals together to gauge whether anyone was worth keeping on, and when I learned she hadn't bothered to ask you, I told her to correct her mistake."

I hugged a cushion to me. "This is so bizarre. Do you want a cup of tea or something?"

"No. But I'd like to offer you a job."

"Not Marni's job?"

"No. Carolyn Stewart is taking over as editor."

"Oh, is she, now? You slimeball."

"I didn't sleep with her, if that's what you're thinking. She's not my type."

I smiled in a know-it-all fashion. He got it, and smiled back. "Not that I have a type."

"So, what's the job, then?" I hugged the cushion closer, gripped by the irrational fear that I was about to be offered the mistress role, complete with a penthouse apartment, mink coat, chauffeur-driven limo, and a few dozen silk brocade cheong-sams.

"Well," he said, "it's to do with new product development . . . ," and he proceeded to explain.

When he was done his description and had answered some of my more basic questions, I said, "What about Helen? She could use a radical change of scene."

"Is she talented?"

"You think I'd be asking if she wasn't?"

"I'm sure we could work something out."

"Regardless?"

"Regardless."

I pushed the cushion aside. "So, that's it?"

"That's it. Think about it. Let me know."

"By when?"

A grin. "Noon tomorrow."

"Oh yeah. Lots of time."

"I'd best be going."

I walked to the door and held it open. "Well, thanks for coming, I guess."

"Rosie?"

"Yes?"

His arm slid around my waist and pulled me close enough to smell his cologne and feel his chest against my collarbone. He bent his head and started kissing me behind the ear.

Uh oh, again. My head started to loll back, and the old familiar Brian lust stole over me, fast and furious. Only it was force of habit as much as anything — my body might have gone into reflex mode, but my head knew I didn't want to sex it up with Brian. For real. So I stiffened, and he noticed right away that for a change I wasn't melting like a cheap candle. He let go.

I straightened my T-shirt and shorts. "How can I even consider working for you if you're going to be making passes at me? You, a married man."

He stepped out the door. "Quite right. My abject apologies. Good-night."

I turned out the lights, brushed my teeth, removed the shorts, climbed into bed. And closed my eyes.

So. Working for Brian. There's a concept. Me, in Jil Sander, sitting in a first class airplane seat beside him, conferring, pointing to the screen of my Powerbook to illustrate how our new products are developing, and trying not to hear the siren-call of the cords of his neck there, where he's undone his top shirt button and loosened his tie.

Stop. Too frightening. Try again.

Okay. Let's look at the TV show idea. How about that one: there I am in the studio, wearing something severe and black, hair pulled into a chignon, carrying a clipboard. And there's Marni, in camera-friendly periwinkle blue, sitting on a high stool. A sound technician attaches her microphone, a makeup artist powders her face, a hair-stylist sprays her hair. Marni snaps her fingers, I jump and run over to her. She asks me a question. I give her an answer. She doesn't like it. She treats me to a withering stare —

Aaagh! Double stop.

I don't know. Maybe someone like Ann Hambleton has the right idea — doing something completely different, something *not* involving fashion or clothes. Though the idea of working retail, of waiting on customers, even for furniture — I shudder to think.

Still. I could picture this Wood Paint store in a big loft space downtown, the interior designed very groovy by someone like Paul Yamaguchi, with apricot-coloured walls, golden wood floors — Julie's pieces gleaming under some halogen spotlights.

A painted armoire would open to reveal little wooden boxes painted in jewel tones sitting on its shelves. And perhaps some fine linens, tied up with grosgrain ribbon, peeking out of an open drawer.

And it would be really cool if Julie could give furniture-painting lessons there, too, in a workshop space. And maybe Max could help set up a small café area, with some good coffee and a few fancy sand-wiches, some fresh-baked chocolate walnut cookies available daily for elevenses . . .

I open my eyes. 1:19. This is getting ridiculous. I sit up, turn on the light, and walk out to the living room. I pull my dope box out from its hiding place behind the bookshelf, quickly roll a joint and light up. What I need to do now, if I ever want to fall asleep, is to replace these obsessive thoughts with restful ones — there was an article about this once in *Panache*.

Okay. So. What's restful and relaxing? Come on, I must be able to think of something. How about the seashore? Visualize a beach, feel a warm summer breeze, add the keening cry of seagulls, the healing pound of the waves —

Wait. Stop. I *hate* the beach. Every time I'm in Florida I'm like, Do we have to? All that sand.

SO THINK OF SOMETHING ELSE, THEN.

All right. Stick with the soft summer breeze, leave the water there, only make it not ocean, but lake. Good so far. And be sailing.

I take a deep drag on the joint. Yeah. Sailing. Me and Max, curled up at the stern of the boat, like Bing Crosby and Grace Kelly in *High Society*. Better still, like Cary Grant and Katharine Hepburn in *Philadelphia Story*.

Or like me and Brian planing in Toronto harbour.

Hit the buzzer. Erase all men from the boat. Try to feel that breeze again. Hey, I almost can, but that's because the top of my head has lifted off — the dope must be taking effect. I stub out the joint in the ashtray and climb back into bed, shut my eyes, sink into my pillows.

Yes, there I am, *alone* on deck, wearing shorts and a T-shirt and looking good — check that muscle tone in the thighs. Very impressive! When'd I do that weight work?

CAN WE HAVE A LITTLE CONCENTRATION HERE?

Fine.

There I am, clipping along at a good speed. The wind's moderate, the sun is sending happy glints to dance on the ruffled water. I hold the tiller in one hand, grasp the mainsheet firmly in the other, and squint at the horizon, steering the boat towards my destination. There I go, eyes ahead, intent on my course . . .

I drift off, happy.